Hunchback

RANDALL WRIGHT

Hunchback

WITHDRAWN

Henry Holt and Company
New York

Henry Holt and Company, LLC
Publishers since 1866
115 West 18th Street
New York, New York 10011
www.henryholt.com

Henry Holt is a registered trademark of Henry Holt and Company, LLC
Copyright © 2004 by Randall Wright
All rights reserved.
Distributed in Canada by H. B. Fenn and Company Ltd.

Library of Congress Cataloging-in-Publication Data
Wright, Randall.
Hunchback / Randall Wright.
p.   cm.
Summary: Thirteen-year-old Hodge, a hunchback orphan living in Castle
Marlby, dreams of serving a prince, and when his wish comes true he
becomes embroiled in adventure and intrigue.
[1. Adventure and adventurers—Fiction.   2. People with disabilities—Fiction.
3. Orphans—Fiction.   4. Princes—Fiction.   5. Kings, queens, rulers, etc.—Fiction.]
I. Title.
PZ7.W95825Hs 2004   [Fic]—dc22   2003056577

ISBN 0-8050-7232-2 / EAN 978-0-8050-7232-7
First Edition—2004
Designed by Amy Manzo Toth
Printed in the United States of America on acid-free paper. ∞

1   3   5   7   9   10   8   6   4   2

For Sissy,
who will always be my little girl

Hunchback

PART I

Castle Marlby

Faith, find a welcome here.

CHAPTER ONE

*H*odge sat in a doorway and trimmed his toenails with a knife.

With one eye turned to the task at hand, he fixed his other eye upon the stone arch directly across the cluttered courtyard. It was a talent he had, this wall-eyed staring, which allowed him to stand on the castle wall and survey both the outer plains and the inner keep at once—to see both the sky and the ground beneath.

Martin's Mary crossed the shadowed square before his view, lugging a bucket of water from the well. Bert the ostler, still in his nightshirt, leaned out from the stable and spit into the courtyard. Young Jayne Kemp, a scullery maid, carried a pail of kitchen scraps to the swine-cote. But for these, the castle might have been abandoned.

Long ago, on a bright summer morning such as this, the keep would have been a much busier place, full of noise and color, sights and smells: the shouting of peddlers, acrobats, and jugglers; the aromas of fresh-baked breads and roasting meats; the officious trumpeting of the royal guard as they heralded the coming of kings and princes. But the castle had long since lost its position of importance to those kings and princes, and was now a place of quiet indolence. Cast-off rubbish littered the courtyard. Tufts of stunted grass peeked up through cracks in the paving stones. Even the bird-soiled towers and battlements seemed to have forgotten those former days of glory.

On many a fire-lit night Hodge had listened in rapt attention as old Jesper told of those times—the days when Castle Marlby had served as a seasonal retreat for the royal family. Rumors hinted that perhaps a return to those olden-golden days was near.

With an impatient sigh, Hodge turned a wandering eye to the sky and then back to the archway. His brother, Fleet, had accused him of wishful thinking, but still those rumors pounded through his heart and filled him with hope.

He pushed himself to his feet and tucked his knife into the belt he always wore cinched about his middle. Standing, his head and shoulders reached no higher than a child's. Though the growth of more than thirteen summers was bound up in his frame, those years had drawn his sinews tight, bowing his back like a willow branch.

He stretched his aching muscles the best he could—he had been crouched in the doorway through the night, and his arms and legs had cramped from the waiting. He shifted from one foot to the other. Scanning the courtyard, he picked out a paving stone to signify the anticipated hour. When the retreating shadow touched its edge, he decided, the royal party would cross the drawbridge, pass through the gatehouse, and enter the inner ward where they could cast off the dust and fatigue of their long journey. And Hodge would approach, bent in his eternal posture of humility, and beg to be of service to the prince himself.

Hodge sniffed the air. He breathed in the early morning smells of damp earth and mildew. Sunlight edged onto his selected stone. The royal party did not appear. He picked out another stone and continued the wait. He slumped back in the doorway, scratched his toes, and yawned. He selected yet another stone. The sun climbed toward noon, and still the courtyard remained in silence except for the uneven squawking of a chicken.

✦ ✦ ✦

It was just yesterday morning that Hodge first heard of the rumored arrival. He was cleaning out the gong pit beneath the castle latrines, an odious job that always left a foul smell on his clothes. He had just splashed a bucket of clean water down the shaft that led to the moat when he heard echoing words from far above. Someone was in the privy.

"I don't know," came a voice, ringing off the stones of the latrine chute. "Maybe it's true."

Sir William, Hodge thought.

"Hah! What would the prince be doing here?" said a second.

Beauchamp?

"I only know what I heard," said a third.

Sir Robert for sure. It's getting awful crowded up there. And then Hodge thought he'd better clear out before those men got down to business. It wasn't until he slogged into the sunlit bailey that he gave attention to what they had said.

A prince? Coming here? It would be a dream come true.

Hodge spied Tom Dalby, the chandler's boy, hustling around the corner of the keep.

"Hey, Tom!" he called, following after him. "Have you heard?"

He rounded the corner just in time to see Tom and Jayne Kemp huddled together by the well. It looked as if they had been kissing. Hodge blushed and backed away, but Tom sniffed the air.

"What's that *smell*?" He pinched his nose and looked about in disgust. "Oh, it's just the gong farmer. Hey, boy, why don't you go where you belong, out with the pigs?"

"Oh, Tom," Jayne said. "Let him be."

Tom picked up a stone. "Hie thee hence," he said, imitating Lord Selden's booming voice. "Get ye gone." He flicked the stone at Hodge, but it clattered harmlessly at his feet.

Hodge snatched up the stone.

"Hey, now, hold there," Tom said, inching back behind Jayne.

"Now Tom," she said.

"I'll not have that fool a-knocking off me head." Pushing Jayne before him as a shield, Tom hustled to safety.

Hodge hurled the stone at the old oak bucket. With a loud *thunk*, the bucket wobbled on the stone wall. A louder *thunk* and the bucket tumbled into the well, trailing its rope behind.

Hodge spun about to see who had thrown the second stone.

Jayne wiped her hands on her skirt. "Better the bucket than Tom's head," she said, and off she dashed after Tom.

Hodge peeked around the corner just in time to see her skipping down the steps into the kitchen. "I'd rather it *was* Tom's head," he said to himself. Then he hurried off to find someone else to tell the news.

"Ho, Bert," he called to the ostler, who was busy pitching hay in the stables.

"Ho, yerself," Bert said. "You been in the sewage again. You better get outta here 'fore you kill my horses with that stench."

"But I just heard that the prince is coming."

"Yeh, and once't I seen a gatehouse flying with the pigs. Now clear out."

Hodge ducked the forkload of hay that Bert tossed at him and scuttled off in search of his brother. But even Fleet didn't seem interested in his news.

"Brother," Fleet said as he braided feathers into a falcon lure, "the prince wouldn't be coming here." He hung up the lure alongside the assorted hoods and jesses that decorated the rear wall of the mews. "Castle Marlby is not important enough for a royal visit."

"But I heard—"

Fleet laughed. "Rumors from the gong pit? Besides, what would it have to do with us even if it were true?"

Hodge kicked at the straw. "Only, I always thought—"

"Yes, I know. You always thought you would like to serve a king. But Hodge, you are the son of a nobody. Like me. What chance do we have?"

"At least you belong to the mews."

"I know, brother. And someday you'll belong to something, too. But first you ought to bathe. You stink a bit."

With Fleet's words tugging at him, Hodge left the mews and trudged across the courtyard, through the gatehouse, and across the fields toward the Eiderlee. He splashed into the icy stream, trying to wash the foul smell from his hair and clothes.

✦ ✦ ✦

Hodge awoke to Fleet's gentle prodding.

"There you are," Fleet said. "Bilda's been looking for you."

Hodge scrabbled about in his mind trying to remember where he was. At last, the memory of paving stones and drowsy waiting crept back into his head. He rubbed his face with a calloused hand. "Awww, what's she want today?"

"She's mucking out the ovens this afternoon," Fleet answered. "She's wanting your help."

"Why this afternoon?"

"In case the rumors be true," Fleet said.

"I thought you didn't believe 'em."

"*I'm* not the one mucking out the ovens."

Hodge pulled on his shabby boots. "My feet's asleep," he groaned, struggling to stand. He tried to stamp the tingling from his toes.

"I think your head's asleep, too," Fleet said. "At least the part between your ears." He helped Hodge steady himself. "Come on, brother. There's work to be done."

Hodge looked up into Fleet's thin face. "And always me to do it."

Fleet chuckled. "Yes, brother, always you." He led the way toward the kitchen with Hodge hobbling along behind, still trying to wiggle the tingling from his toes.

"Wait up," Hodge called.

✦ ✦ ✦

Though Lord Selden was by lineage the most important person in the castle, many of its inhabitants secretly deferred to Bilda, the cook. She was the largest person in the keep—evidence of her culinary skills, which gave her a status slightly higher than nobility. To Hodge, however, she was simply a bothersome taskmistress. Because of his deformity, he was of scant use to the ostler or the blacksmith. All he was good for was hauling wood, cleaning the privies—and mucking out the ovens.

"There you are," Bilda said.

Hodge stumbled down the steps into the kitchen, leaving Fleet to get back to his own duties in the mews. With the midday meal finished, the kitchen was nearly empty now. Bilda thrust a large, wooden pail into Hodge's hands.

"The pastry oven first," she said.

He grunted, but accepted the bucket. With a rake he pulled the ashes from the trough beneath. Leftover warmth from the morning baking caused beads of sweat to break out on his brow. He filled the bucket, carried it to the barrow waiting just outside the kitchen door, and dumped it in a gray flurry of ashes.

Tom Dalby sauntered by and knocked the bucket from his hands. "Still to your eyeballs in filth?" he asked. Then he laughed and hurried away.

Hodge scowled. He wondered how anyone could say Tom was near old enough to be called a man. Grumbling, Hodge returned to the kitchen to fill the bucket again.

Once the trough was cleared and swept, he leaned into the oven proper to scrape the floor and walls. By the time he pulled himself back out he was drenched with sweat. He could taste the salt on his lips.

"Are you done?" Bilda asked, looking up from the dinner preparations.

Her question made Hodge think of the baking bread. He wiped his face with the back of his arm. "I'm well done."

"Good." Bilda flung several chunks of coney meat into a boiling pot. "Now for the other."

Hodge groaned. Fat drippings from a year's worth of oxen, boar, and mutton were waiting to be shoveled from the large oven. A messy task made worse by the grease-slippery stones. It was almost as bad as cleaning the latrines. After a moment's hesitation, Hodge heaved himself inside. He grimaced at the rancid smell. This oven was big enough to roast three oxen standing side by side, with room yet to run a bit, if the urge took them. Hodge could stand inside it well enough. He pushed his shovel into the muck and sliced up a pile of congealed fat and ash. The shovel struck the back wall with a *thunk*.

He scraped the muck off his shovel into the bucket and set himself for another pass, but a booming voice echoed through the kitchen. Lord Selden's voice. Hodge turned a free eye to the oven door.

"We must have a feast!" Lord Selden boomed.

"Yes, m'Lord," Bilda answered.

"Tomorrow," he boomed again.

"Yes, m'Lord."

"I have received a letter. With the royal seal. The prince *is* coming. We will have a boar or two. And doves. And liver and kidney pies. And sweetlings and honey breads. And we'll crack a new cask in the buttery so we have plenty to drink."

"Yes, m'Lord."

Hodge peeked from the oven in time to see Bilda's brief curtsy to Lord Selden's back. The Lord of the Castle disappeared out the door, hurrying on to other boomings.

"It's true?" Hodge asked, climbing out of the oven.

Bilda nodded. "Seems it's so." She threw another chunk of coney meat into the stew. "And who is going boar hunting this late in the day, I'd like to know?"

✦ ✦ ✦

That night Hodge lay curled up in the straw of their tower basement next to Fleet. Some vermin-pest was chewing on the back of his knee. He scratched at it only to make the stinging worse. Giving up, he pulled his blanket over his shoulders. "I was wrong," he said to his brother, trying to keep the excitement out of his voice.

"Mmmm." Fleet seemed half asleep.

"The prince is not coming today."

"Mmmmm."

"Yes, I was wrong." Hodge pulled the blanket close to hide his gloating. "He's coming tomorrow!"

"So I heard."

Hodge rolled himself up to a sitting position. "You heard? From who?"

Fleet answered from the depths of his own bedding. "It's buzzing about the whole of the keep. Lord Selden had the butler jumping about like Beelzebub was on his tail."

Hodge flopped back to his side. "Well . . . I heard it from m'Lord himself."

"Oh? And what did he tell you, brother?"

"That he got a letter with the royal seal. The prince *is* coming, and he'll be here tomorrow. There'll be a feast. But Bilda says no boar. It's to be mutton."

"Mutton? That's a bit common for a prince."

"Well . . . maybe there'll be an ox. Or two."

"Then it surely will be a feast."

Hodge nodded in the dark. "A fine feast. And I will offer the prince my service. *He* will have a use for me."

"Well, brother, he might. And I hope he does, if he really comes. But now it's late. Go to sleep."

Hodge could hear Fleet rustling to a comfortable spot. And then there was silence.

"Good night," Hodge whispered.

CHAPTER TWO

*T*he castle had not seen such bustle for many a year. It seemed Lord Selden wanted everything done at once: the scattering of fresh rushes and lavender in the Hall; weeding and cleaning of the inner ward; mucking out the stables, dovecotes, and mews—all things with which Hodge could help. For once, he didn't mind. And for once, even Tom Dalby was too busy to torment him.

Hodge hurried about the castle in high excitement, skittering from place to place. He offered his hand at hauling wood for the great fireplace in the solar, Lord Selden's private quarters above the hall. He begged to help with the repairs of the drawbridge. He insisted he be allowed to climb the High Tower to watch for the royal party. Then he hurried away to the kitchen on some pretext, that he might only breathe in the smells of Bilda's banquet preparations.

There was neither boar nor ox, only mutton and twenty peacocks roasting slowly on spits over the open hearth. Hodge's mouth watered. His stomach growled. Normally dinner would have been served at noon, with the sun high in the sky. But today it would await the arrival of the prince. A pilfered bite of bread would have to sustain Hodge till then.

"Get you gone, boy," Bilda said. "You're underfoot something dreadful today. Go help in the Hall."

Jayne Kemp pressed a hunk of cheese into his hand and hurried him toward the door. "She's a terror today," she whispered. "Better to keep clear if you can."

And so he was off again, searching for another place he might be of assistance.

At midafternoon he ran into Fleet coming from the mews.

"There you are, brother," Fleet said. "How goes the waiting?"

"Slow," Hodge said. "Slow, slow, and slow." He looked up at Fleet. "Is there any news?"

Fleet shook his head. "None. Perhaps we'll have to feast without the prince."

"No!" Then Hodge saw the smile on Fleet's face. "You're teasing me."

"Only a bit. Don't you worry. Perhaps they're crossing the Eiderlee even now."

"Yes, and coming up the valley."

Fleet nodded. "Horses' hooves still damp from the stream."

"Across the causeway."

"Over the moat."

"Through the gate."

"They're here!" Fleet said.

Hodge glanced across the courtyard, looking to see if their words had made it so. A pair of yellow butterflies danced around each other in the glimmering air. All else was still.

"Patience," Fleet said.

"Well, they'd better hurry, or the peacocks will be all burned up."

✦ ✦ ✦

To Hodge's dismay, Fleet's words proved prophetic—the feast *was* held without the prince. The afternoon passed with no sign of the royal party. The bustling anticipation that had filled the castle slowly ebbed, fading along with the dying day. Finally, Lord Selden ordered a halt to the preparations. He stood in the courtyard and boomed out his thanks to everyone. And, he said, since they had all worked so hard, they deserved to be fed. So as the sun settled in the west, the Hall echoed with the clatter and chatter of a banquet without a guest. Talk of the prince soon gave way to interest in meatier matters—namely mutton, fowl, and fish.

From the lowest knave to Lord Selden himself, they each dug into the feast with relish. And each retired that night with a belly full to bursting. Hodge, however, had ingested a good, round helping of disappointment along with the honey breads. Though his stomach was full, he burrowed into his straw bed with an empty heart.

"The prince didn't come," he whispered.

"No," Fleet said, yawning. "He didn't."

With a whoosh of wings a dark owl swept down from the rafters above and out into the night. "Good hunting," Hodge mumbled. In addition to the owl, he and his brother shared the basement floor of their corner tower with three cats, a family of swallows, and a multitude of other uncounted, unseen creatures.

"Maybe tomorrow?" Hodge asked.

But Fleet's breathing came steady and slow.

"Maybe," Hodge said, answering his own question. He nestled farther down into the straw. Soon he, too, fell asleep with the *maybe* echoing in his mind.

✦ ✦ ✦

When Hodge awoke the next morning he could feel the change. There was something in the air—a smell, a feeling, a wisp of breeze, a clattering echo. He pulled on his boots and hurried out. Fleet had already gone.

Hodge looked about as he crossed the courtyard, trying to see what he had already sensed. The signs were there for his reading: strange horses in the stable, their noses buried in fresh-piled hay; men-at-arms in unfamiliar livery stalking across the ward; the portcullis down; the drawbridge up. The prince was here! He must have arrived sometime in the night. Excited, Hodge glanced at the Hall. New colors flew from its height: a banner of yellow and red flapped in the morning breeze. Hodge could hear it snapping as it caught the wind.

But then his excitement faltered. This wasn't what he had imagined. In his daydreams the prince had ridden through the gates on a white charger. His retinue had marched behind on jet-black steeds, accompanied by the musical clank of weapons and rattling bridles, straight out of one of Jesper's stories. Hodge would be the first to greet them. "Welcome, Sire," he would say. "Welcome to Castle Marlby."

The prince would be impressed by his humility.

"And who might you be?" he would ask.

"Hodge, son of Rolf. Your servant."

With a hand on Hodge's shoulder, the prince would say, "My servant you shall be."

But it had happened all wrong. The prince and all his men had arrived in the dead of night without any fanfare or panoply. Hodge had slept like a corpse through the stamp and clatter of horses' hooves, the squeal of the lowering portcullis, the squawk of the rising drawbridge, and the windblown flap of the newly posted colors.

"Pah!" he said to himself. "I sleep too much."

He cast another glance at the Hall. There, Lord Selden and the prince would likely be deep in counsel, discussing the many and varied affairs of nobility. In disappointment Hodge started across the inner ward, intent on the way things should have been. He stopped in surprise as Lord Selden appeared from the Hall and scurried toward the stables with the prince's man-at-arms at his side. Lord Selden's normal booming sounded muffled and uncertain.

The drawbridge rattled and clanked as it was lowered into place beyond the rising portcullis. The prince's man jumped astride a mottled gray horse and reined it toward the gates. With a kick to its flank, the horse leaped forward through the gatehouse and clattered over the drawbridge.

And then, just as quickly, the drawbridge was raised, the portcullis lowered, and the gates closed.

✦ ✦ ✦

There was to be no grand feast that day. Though the prince had taken up residence in the solar above the Great Hall, no banquet was being held to honor his presence. Hodge wondered if they had been rash to prepare so heartily the day before, only to have it wasted on an empty throne.

Without a banquet, Hodge would have scant chance to meet the prince. He said as much to the ostler's cat. "But," he added, surprised at his own ingenuity, "the prince does have to eat." He glanced at the sun overhead. "Soon enough!" He raced to the Hall, arriving just in time for the noonday meal.

As always, Fleet had saved him a place. Hodge wormed his way onto the bench between his brother and Mrs. Belcher, the weaver's woman. At nose level with the table, he dipped a hunk of bread into his steaming bowl of stew.

"Where is he?" he asked, keeping his voice low so no one would overhear. He tore a bite from the sopping bread.

"Who?" Fleet whispered back.

"The prince."

"Ahhh. That's the mystery. Seems his horse is here, but maybe he isn't."

Hodge swallowed hard. "What?"

"No one's seen him."

Hodge dropped his bread into his bowl. "But the royal banner . . . ?"

Fleet shrugged.

"And his men?"

Mrs. Belcher shifted on the bench, reaching across the table for the pitcher of drink.

Hodge lowered his voice again. "And his men?"

"Yes, his men are here," Fleet said. "Leastwise I believe they're his men. But they don't seem too friendly. And they're not just armed. They're *carrying* their weapons. Like they might want to use them. They've got old Sir Granby at odds. Our own men-at-arms don't seem to know what to do. They're standing around like they've just lost their best girls."

"Maybe it's secret business."

"It's well guarded if it is."

Hodge kept a single eye on his brother and let the other scan the hall. "Where do the prince's men dine?"

"On their feet, it appears."

"I saw one of them leave," Hodge said. "Off like a bolt on some errand."

Fleet chewed quietly for a moment. "One thing I'd like to know," he said at last. "Why are we closed up so tight, as if for a siege?"

"A siege?"

"Yes. Can you even remember the last time the bridge was up and the gates closed and no one allowed in or out?"

"No one?"

"Not a soul. No one except the prince's man."

CHAPTER THREE

*R*umors swirled about the castle in gusts and eddies. Hodge heard from Jayne Kemp that an unknown illness wracked the prince's body, keeping him in his room, where he drank potions and tonics and prayed for healing.

Fleet's master, Bram the falconer, told the brothers that the prince was a staggering drunkard. Just last night, he said, his Royal Highness tried to leave his quarters only to get lost in the oratory, thinking it was the privy.

The ostler, on the other hand, indicated he knew for a fact that the prince's stallion had arrived riderless. When pressed, however, he admitted that he had not been completely coherent when the party entrusted their mounts to his care late that night.

The prince's men were close-lipped, and Lord Selden seemed hesitant to offer any explanations—if indeed he had any. In fact, the newly arrived force of arms had taken over the castle as if it were their own, limiting movement to only those whose comings and goings were vital to castle operation. And throughout all this the prince remained invisible—secluded in his quarters or even missing altogether.

As a little boy, Hodge had grown accustomed to leaving the castle grounds whenever he cared to. Even now, because his duties were light, he would often slip out and wade through the fields of ripening grain or clamber up into the wild hills to the west. Through his exploration, he had learned much about the surrounding countryside. He knew by name even the very youngest of the villagers in the town across the meadow. He had discovered caves way back upon the wooded slopes beyond the castle. He found deep pools in the Eiderlee that proved to be full of trout. He prided himself that he knew more of the country round about than most inhabitants of the castle. So naturally when he became weary of waiting for the prince to appear, he thought he might stretch his legs a bit in the outside world.

He headed toward the gatehouse, his mind fixed on the undulating fish in their deep pools. Guards in red and yellow livery stood at the gate, cruel-looking pikes planted at their sides. They kept silent watch as Hodge approached.

He looked past them at the closed gate. Though he stepped forward with clear intention to leave the castle, neither man moved to pull the bolts. He stopped with one eye fixed on the guard to his left. With the other he looked up at the tower. He didn't recognize the man who stood high on the battlement.

"Well," he said. "I can't open it myself."

The guard didn't blink.

Hodge turned to the burly fellow on his right. "Can you help me?"

Barely a threatening twitch from the corners of his mouth, and then he was still.

Hodge shrugged and stepped forward. He jerked to a halt as twin pikes crossed before his nose.

"State your business," growled the burly guard.

Hodge staggered back. "I—I just wanted to go down to the brook."

The pikes remained crossed. "You have not been given leave."

✦ ✦ ✦

Hodge went straight to the mews. He found Fleet back amongst the perches, feeding bits of pigeon to a small peregrine falcon. The bird wore a hood that covered its head and eyes, but left its beak free for tearing.

"You're lucky to be working here," Hodge said.

Fleet smiled, though he kept his eyes on the bird. "Not if he takes my finger."

Hodge shrugged. "I wish I could work with the falcons." Though he enjoyed his free rein of the castle, he had always been a bit envious of his brother.

"Don't worry. You'll be serving the prince soon enough, remember?"

Hodge grunted. And then he told Fleet of his experience at the gate.

"Hmmm." Fleet wiped his hands on his leather apron. "Seems to me they're guarding the wrong side of the wall."

"What do you mean?"

"Why would guards be posted on the inside of a closed gate? Are they afraid of escape?"

Hodge laughed. "Escape from what?"

"I don't know," Fleet answered. "This is all very strange."

✦ ✦ ✦

With the arrival of the prince's party, the nature of life in the castle had changed. The slow and easy days had become suddenly businesslike and uncommonly efficient. Hodge found his accustomed freedom stifled by the presence of watchmen at every turn. He spent his time wandering from the kitchens to the stables and mews, avoiding the guards at the gate and Hall. He came to realize he was not alone in his feelings of confinement. They seemed to be shared by the whole of the castle.

Though hardly voiced, the complaints and grumbles manifested themselves in other ways—in shortened tempers, sullen looks, and subdued chatter, even in the Hall during the dinner meal. Only Bilda in the kitchen seemed to speak her displeasure aloud. She grumbled while she cut, chopped, and cooked. She complained about the difficulty of obtaining herbs, the unnatural feeling of watchfulness, the absence of jollity in the evenings. Which made Hodge laugh, because Bilda was seldom jolly at all. She scolded him for being underfoot in the busy kitchen.

"Here, do something useful," she said. She dropped a loaf of bread onto an earthenware tray alongside a roasted capon and onions. "Take this to the prince." She covered it with a steaming towel to keep in the warmth.

"Who, me? To the prince?"

"To his guards. They'll see he gets it."

Hodge clutched the tray in his arms, his chest swelling with importance.

"Don't drop it!" Bilda said. "Or I'll bake you in a pie."

With great care (and not because of Bilda's warning) Hodge carried his burden toward the Hall, walking slowly through the buttery and up the short steps. He paused before the guard stationed at the door to the Hall.

"For the prince," he proclaimed in a loud voice. "His dinner."

The guard signaled for him to continue.

He entered the Hall. The two soldiers who stood at the foot of the wide stairs barred the way with their pikes.

"The prince's dinner," Hodge said.

They allowed him to proceed.

He climbed the stairs, still cautious with his burden. When he reached the top step, however, he faltered. At the end of the long corridor, two more guards stood posted at the entrance to the solar, where the prince would be waiting his dinner. The prince! Hodge approached under the guards' unwavering gaze. He grew more and more nervous with each step he took.

Finally, he halted before them. "Dinner for His Majesty?" he said, feeling timid and small.

The guard on the left lifted a corner of the towel, just far enough to peek inside without having to tip his head. He turned sharply and struck the door twice.

The door squeaked open, revealing another man in guard livery. He examined Hodge from head to foot, his gaze lingering on Hodge's bent back and hunched shoulders. Without a word, he took the tray and retreated into the room, closing the door behind him.

Hodge stood in silence. The guards on either side of the door made no move to dismiss him. But for their breathing they might have been statues—statues arrayed in chain mail and the yellow and red of the royal family.

Hodge raced back to the kitchen to report to Bilda that there would be no Hodge pie that afternoon. And from that day on, he arrived just in time for Bilda to entrust him with the prince's meals.

✦ ✦ ✦

As the days turned into a week, then two, the new routine gradually insinuated itself into castle life. The ever-present guards and invisible prince became accepted fixtures. Even Bilda grew tired of complaining and returned to running the kitchen with her normal chaotic fussing, ordering about the scullery maids and serving girls with brusque commands.

Though he still had yet to meet the prince, Hodge had settled happily into his new role.

"This is what you wanted," Fleet said to him one evening after they retired to their tower basement. "To serve the prince."

Hodge nodded. The owl had just swept down from its perch to soar out into the night. "Good hunting," Hodge whispered. He lay back on the straw. "I should still like to see him, though."

Fleet turned quiet.

Hodge thought he must have fallen asleep. "Good night," he whispered.

Fleet sat up. "You know, this royal visit is certainly different from the stories Jesper has told."

Hodge shrugged. "The prince likes quiet," he said.

"Maybe so. But it seems to me these men-at-arms are more like jailers than royal guards."

"What do you mean? Why would we be kept as prisoners?"

"It's not us I'm thinking of."

"Well, I meant Lord Selden and all of us."

"Nor him neither."

"What?"

"I'm not sure." Fleet fell back to his bed. "I'm just the falcon boy. How would I know anything?" He pulled his blanket up over his shoulders and rolled to his side. "Now go to sleep."

Hodge stared into the darkness, thinking of what Fleet had said. "Jailers? For who? That's silly."

CHAPTER FOUR

*I*t was during the third week of the "occupation" (as Fleet had come to call it) that Hodge finally caught a glimpse of the royal person. Bilda had sent him to deliver a breakfast of bread and cheese. The now-familiar guard took the platter and turned back through the open door. Hodge spied a man beyond, pacing the floor. A youngish man with dark hair and a closely cropped beard.

The man paused in the center of the room. Even from that distance, Hodge could see bright blue eyes staring back at him.

"Who are you?" the man called.

But the guard had already begun to close the door.

"No, wait a moment, Findley," the man said.

"Your Highness," the guard replied in a stern tone.

The bang of the closing door echoed along the corridor.

From inside the room Hodge heard a muffled voice say, "What harm could *he* do?"

And then there was silence. Hodge became conscious of the other guards standing on either side.

"Was that the prince?" he asked. But the guards' silence made him answer his own question. "It must be." He rushed to tell Fleet.

He had to temper his excitement upon finding Lord Selden in the mews. Bram, the master falconer, stood with him, extolling the virtues of the peregrine falcon he held on his arm. "An elegant bird," he said, "especially when compared to the kestrel."

Lord Selden's booming voice replied, "Ah, what odds does it make? I can't take 'em out hunting, now can I?"

Hodge ducked back along the near wall and found Fleet at the workbench, patching the hood of an old tiercel. Even with his hood removed, the bird perched docilely on the table, looking about with his one good eye. His other eye had been lost in a hunting accident several years earlier. He wasn't of much sporting use now, but Lord Selden was loath to get rid of the ancient falcon.

"Old Titus here has been growing restless of late," Fleet whispered. "I do believe he misses the chase."

Lord Selden's voice echoed through the rafters. "It's preposterous that I can't even take my own birds out." He stormed from the mews with Bram following close behind.

"Seems m'Lord misses it, too," Fleet added. Then he turned to Hodge. "How, now, brother?"

Hodge stroked Titus's soft-feathered breast, trying to act calm and unruffled himself. "I've seen the prince," he said in what he hoped was a steady voice.

"Have you?"

"Yes. He even asked my name. Ouch!" Titus had nipped his finger.

"Here," Fleet said, handing Hodge pieces of rabbit. "He's hungry."

Hodge parceled out the bits of meat to the bird, wary now of the sharp beak. "The prince is very tall," he said. "And dark haired, with blue eyes like water."

"Oh? Did he appear at all ill? Or drunk?"

Hodge shook his head. "Nah. He looked fine to me."

Fleet smiled. "Or invisible?"

"No! Nor that neither!"

They both laughed.

"Brother," Fleet said, "you'll make your fortune. You've seen the prince, and he's asked your name."

Hodge nodded in satisfaction.

✦ ✦ ✦

When Hodge arrived with the midday meal, there appeared to be an argument brewing beyond the solar door. Though the guard had already rapped to announce dinner, the door did not immediately open and voices seemed to be battling back and forth inside the room.

Hodge stared uncomfortably at the floor. The guard knocked again. The voices continued, one rising in volume until Hodge could plainly hear it.

"That is what I want," the voice said. "That is what I command." And then there was silence.

The door squeaked open. The guard, Findley, looked down at Hodge. "Bring the meal in," he said in a tight voice. "His Highness would like some company."

Hodge felt rooted to the spot. He had the confused impression that he had been asked to enter the room, but that couldn't be right.

"Hurry up," Findley said. "The meat will be cold."

Still dazed, Hodge shuffled forward while the man held the door.

"What are you called?" Findley asked.

Hodge just managed to stammer out his name.

"Hodge?" repeated Findley.

"Hodge. Son of Rolf."

Findley closed the door and snapped to attention. With a voice formal and loud, he cried, "Your Highness, I present to you Hodge, son of Rolf." Then he bowed. "Hodge, son of Rolf, I present to you Prince Leo, eldest son of his Royal Majesty, King Alfred the Second, and heir presumptive to the throne."

The prince stood at the window, gazing into the courtyard below. He turned about with a smile starting up on his face. The smile froze, then changed to a look of confusion.

"Who are you?" he asked.

"This is the visitor you requested," Findley answered. "May you enjoy his company."

"What?"

"It was your command. And I obeyed."

"But he's not—" The prince let his unspoken thought dissolve into an angry glare. His eyes reminded Hodge of winter ice on the Eiderlee. "He's nothing but a lackey," the prince said at last.

Findley did not respond.

Hodge still clutched the meal tray in his arms. "Your Highness, I've brought your dinner. Where shall I put it?" He noticed a table to his right—a large oak table, big enough to seat a dozen men. "Is this all right?"

The prince nodded curtly. But then the anger slipped from his face in an easy movement, disappearing as if it had never been there. "What did you bring me today?" A cheerful tone touched the edges of his voice. He lifted the towel from the tray. "Ah, pheasant. And fish. And bread. And apples. At least I eat well. You have an excellent kitchen, *Lord* Hodge."

Hodge placed the tray on the table and stepped away. "I'm not the lord here," he said. "I'm just—"

"Sit," the prince commanded, pulling a chair from the table. "You shall join me."

Hesitantly, Hodge took the offered chair. Prince Leo sat across from him and ladled the food onto trenchers of bread.

"Do you play chess?" the prince asked, looking up.

Because of his bent back, Hodge's eyes barely reached over the massive table. "I can play odds 'n' evens," he said.

"I am not familiar with that game. You will have to teach me sometime, Lord Hodge."

✦ ✦ ✦

Hodge stayed with the prince for a good part of the afternoon, listening in awe as the prince spoke of things both strange and wonderful: boar-hunting in the wild forests of Evinsmore; dining with princesses dressed in gowns of pure silver and gold; taming stallions culled from feral herds. The prince laughingly added that princesses were the most dangerous of the three. Hodge couldn't help but grin at the way Prince Leo spoke to him—as if he were a familiar of equal rank and breeding. Though Hodge squirmed each time the prince called him "Lord," he had given up trying to correct the misunderstanding.

At last Findley coughed loudly, and Prince Leo arose. "We must do this again," he said, escorting Hodge to the door.

Hodge, stooped though he was, bowed even lower. "I will ever be at your service," he said, thrilled to say the words he had practiced to himself so many times.

Prince Leo placed a hand on his shoulder. "My servant you shall be."

Hodge looked up into his face. The royal eyes sparkled.

✦ ✦ ✦

Hodge found his brother drawing water from the well in the far corner of the ward. The well nestled in the angle formed by the inner curtain wall and the keep, and was guarded by stone sides and a shingled roof. With his back to the open court, Fleet strained at the windlass, pulling up a full bucket from the depths. Because of the rattle and squeal of the crank, Hodge was able to sneak up on him without being detected.

"Ho! Brother," he cried.

Fleet jumped and the crank slipped from his hands. Spinning uncontrollably, the windlass uncoiled, and the bucket hurtled back into the well. With an echoing splash, the full bucket hit bottom.

Fleet's face clouded with anger. "Brother—"

Hodge hung his head. "I'm sorry. I didn't mean to startle you." He peeked sheepishly up at Fleet. "I'll help you draw it again."

"No, I'll do it." Fleet grabbed the handle and began turning. After a moment, he glanced over his shoulder at Hodge. "Oh, all right. Come help."

Hodge sprang forward and added his strength to the cranking. "I've news," he shouted over the squeak of the windlass.

"News?"

"I dined with Prince Leo this noontime."

Fleet stared at Hodge. "You what?"

"I dined with the prince. I spent much of the afternoon with him."

"Are you telling me a story?"

"No! The prince wanted company. And I was there. He told me all about—"

"Why would the prince spend the afternoon with you?" Fleet interrupted. "He is of the highest rank, and you are . . . well, you are only Hodge."

Hodge's elation faded. This constant questioning was becoming annoying. "Why, why, why," Hodge repeated. "Why can't you be happy for me?"

"I'm sorry, brother, but I am filled with misgivings. Something mysterious is afoot."

"You're jealous."

"No. I'm your brother, and I'm concerned."

Standing on his toes, Hodge reached for the bucket and hauled it over the well's stone wall. "Here's your water." He dropped the bucket, letting it splash all over the ground. Then he stalked off to the kitchen.

✦ ✦ ✦

The next noon, Hodge was invited into the solar again.

"You were going to teach me a game," said the prince as they finished their meal. "What did you call it?"

"Odds 'n' evens."

"Yes. How is it played? What equipment is needed?"

Hodge peeked over the table. "Just these," he said, holding up both hands and wiggling his fingers.

The prince imitated his action. "Just these?"

"Yes. I call out 'odds' or 'evens,' and we each hold up a number of fingers and count them all. If I called 'odds' and the count is odd, then I win. If the count is even, then you win."

The prince nodded his head. "And then what?"

"Then we play again."

"Oh." The prince smiled. "So elegant in its simplicity."

"Or you can play for money," Hodge offered. "Only I haven't any."

"Then we'll just play for fun."

Not long after, Hodge wished they were playing for money, because he won nearly every round. At first he thought Prince Leo was trying to cheat by slipping an extra finger out at the last second. But that couldn't be—it only happened on rounds that Hodge won.

CHAPTER FIVE

*H*odge loved waiting in the kitchen while Bilda prepared the royal dinner. He delighted in the smells
of cooking: the roasting meats, the baking breads, the
herbs and spices. In addition to the heavenly aromas, the
constant bustle of the kitchen kept Hodge entertained as
he perched upon a stool against the wall. Next to his meal
with the prince, this was the best part of his day.

Today, chickens were roasting on the open hearth, and
from the pastry oven wafted the aroma of venison pies. As
noon approached, the bustle increased. Though the prince
would receive the first hen from the spit and the first of
the pies, after that there was the whole castle to feed.
Hodge sat back and watched the elaborate dance of
pages, maids, and cooks; amazed that no one caught himself afire or chopped off a hand or a head.

In the middle of it all, Bilda signaled to Hodge that the royal meal was ready. He jumped down just as Lord Selden burst through the kitchen door. At once, everything stopped. Every soul froze. Hodge glanced to see if the fires were still burning.

Lord Selden waved his arms. "No, no," he boomed. "Carry on. Carry on." He looked about and spied Hodge. "Come here, my boy."

The activity in the kitchen resumed. The chatter and clamor erupted anew, perhaps even louder than before.

Bilda intercepted Lord Selden as he tried to cross the floor. "M'Lord," she said, "the boy must deliver dinner to the prince."

"Yes, yes. That is why I've come." He looked at Hodge with an appraising air. "And what does he see in you?"

"M'Lord?" Hodge asked.

"It has come to my understanding that you dine with the prince."

Hodge looked at his feet. "Yes, m'Lord."

"Today I will join you." Lord Selden took the tray from Bilda. "Come along," he boomed.

Hodge glanced from the master to the cook.

Bilda shrugged. "Get going," she said.

Lord Selden carried the tray through the buttery, past the guard, and into the Hall. "Well," he said. "And what do you find to talk about with the prince, I wonder?"

Hodge itched to take the tray from Lord Selden. He

skipped to keep up with his master's hurried stride. "His Highness talks, mostly," he said. "But I taught him a game."

"Oh?"

"I taught him odds 'n' evens. I guess I didn't teach him very well. I won nearly every game."

Lord Selden chuckled. "My boy, it is not good to beat the prince at anything."

The guards at the foot of the stairs drew aside to let them pass.

"But what does the prince talk about?" Lord Selden asked.

Hodge leaped ahead a step or two. "Oh, about wonderful things. Things only a prince would know. About princesses and horses. About feasts that make Bilda's cooking look like famine. About—"

"Yes," Lord Selden interrupted. "All those things. But what else?" He lowered his voice. "Has he said why he is here? And why he keeps to himself?"

Hodge jumped to the top step. "No. Why would he tell that to me? But hurry, the food will be cold."

At the entrance to the solar they paused while the guard made his accustomed rap on the door. Findley appeared, looking surprised for an instant, but he quickly recovered himself. "Yes, m'Lord?" he said, addressing Lord Selden.

"We have brought His Majesty's dinner."

"Thank you." Findley took the tray, and as Lord Selden stepped to follow, two pikes snapped before him, nearly catching his nose.

"Only this one may enter," Findley said, nodding at Hodge, who passed easily beneath the dangerous pikes.

The door closed. Findley placed the meal on the table. The prince took his seat and invited Hodge to join him.

"Who was that with you today?" the prince asked.

"Lord Selden, the master of the castle."

"The master of the castle? I thought *you* were the master here."

Hodge could feel himself start to blush. He opened his mouth to protest, but then noticed Prince Leo was smiling.

"You're teasing me," Hodge said. "Just like my brother, Fleet."

The prince bowed his head. "Yes, I suppose I was—just a little game, like your odds 'n' evens. I am sorry." He looked up and sighed. "Since I cannot have noble company, I pretended you were a noble."

"You are the prince. It seems you could have any company you wished."

With a quick glance at Findley, Prince Leo lowered his voice. "These are dangerous times. No one is to be trusted, and so I am protected constantly. Never any peace, nor escape." He sat up straight in his chair and lifted the towel off the tray. "Ah, chicken. And what are these? Venison pies? Who is your cook, m'Lord?"

"I do not like being teased," Hodge replied, starting to feel annoyed.

The prince replaced the cloth on the tray. "I apologize again. I will not tease you further. But since you are not to be Lord of the Castle, tell me who you really are."

"I am Hodge, son of Rolf."

"And who was Rolf?"

"My father. The fletcher."

"An honorable trade. He plies it well?"

"He's dead." Hodge reached for the decanter. "Would you like some wine, Your Highness?" He poured the ruby liquid into a goblet.

The prince accepted the cup and took a long drink. He paused for breath. Then he drank again, tipping his head back. With a thump, he set the empty cup on the table. "My father the king is yet alive." He wiped his mouth on his sleeve. "So, Master Hodge, have *you* been without a father long?"

Hodge had just taken a short sip of wine himself. He swallowed quickly. "Most all my life. I don't remember him or my mother. Fleet, he's my brother, tells me stories of them. My father died of the ague, my mother in childbirth."

Prince Leo handed Hodge a pie. "And what of the baby?"

"What baby?"

"You said your mother died in childbirth."

"Oh. The baby was me."

"You seem to have recovered from your birth."

"Mostly. But it was a long time ago. I don't remember much about it. Fleet says it was more than thirteen summers ago."

"Thirteen summers? Is that all?" Prince Leo wiped dribbled gravy off his chin, smearing it into his short beard. "You seem much older to me. Are you to be a fletcher like your father?"

Hodge squirmed in his chair and accidentally banged the trestle of the table with his boot. Out of the corner of his eye, he saw Findley tense, as if the sound had startled him.

"I can't be a fletcher," Hodge said. "I've not the ability. My brother is to be a falconer, though. He already can sweep a lure as well as Master Bram. I help in the kitchen, but I don't cook."

"You have no trade?"

Hodge shook his head, wishing with all his heart he might say yes. "My back won't straighten out. I can't do much more than simple work."

Prince Leo stared at Hodge with an appraising air. After a moment he said, "Maybe you can do just enough." He refilled his goblet with wine and took another drink. "Maybe just enough. Well, Hodge, son of Rolf. You taught me your game. Perhaps now I should teach you chess."

CHAPTER SIX

*H*odge was in hiding. He had started his lessons at chess, and they were going poorly—he just couldn't keep straight the differences between the Rook, the Knight, and the Bishop. Their respective movements made no sense. In fact, the whole game made no sense. How could the King be more limited than the Queen?

"The King can do anything!" he had said to Prince Leo.

The prince laughed at that, his blue eyes sparkling. He had been more than patient with Hodge. Instead of haranguing him on his incorrect moves, the prince spoke in soft, soothing tones while they played, asking insignificant questions about Castle Marlby and the land round about. He asked whether the castle had a postern. He asked how deep the moat was. He even asked about the latrines and who cleaned them. Hodge absentmindedly answered each question as he stared at the board, trying to remember which piece moved diagonally. He feared he would never master the game. Every evening he left the solar feeling downhearted—disappointed that he was perhaps disappointing the prince.

On top of that, Lord Selden had been angry with him. Ever since the day m'Lord was blocked from entering the prince's chambers, he had been cool and aloof. And just as Lord Selden treated Hodge, so it seemed did the rest of the castle—with impatience and disdain. It was as if everyone had turned into a Tom Dalby. And Tom was even worse than usual, freer in his tormenting.

"Ho! Thou royal boot-licker," Tom yelled to Hodge one morning. "Bring me my breakfast." He sat in the Great Hall with his feet propped on a table.

Hodge had just returned from delivering the morning meal to the prince. He tried to ignore Tom, but it was not easy with so many people about.

"Where's my breakfast, ye dolt-headed serving wench?"

The scattered laughter made Hodge's ears burn. He tried to escape toward the kitchen, but he nearly collided with Jayne Kemp coming up the steps from the buttery, carrying a tray. He jumped back to let her pass.

"Why do you keep company with him?" he muttered under his breath.

"With who?" she asked.

Hodge stuttered in embarrassment. He hadn't meant for her to hear. "Uh, um, that Tom."

Jayne laughed, a bright, sparkling laugh, and pushed her auburn hair out of her face. "Why, who else is there?"

Hodge wanted to say, "What about my brother? Or me?"

"Besides," Jayne continued, "Tom is a dear."

"Maybe to you. You're—" Hodge was going to say *pretty* but stopped himself just in time.

"Jayne," Tom yelled across the Hall, "there's morning in the meadow. We can see it from the tower even if we can't get out in it. Let that slack-wit be."

Jayne set her tray on a nearby table. "I've too much to do," she called back. She began gathering up dirty breakfast dishes. "Maybe Hodge would like to go with you." She smiled.

"Hah!" Tom blurted. "I'll not spend the morning with that gong farmer." He jumped up from the table and disappeared out the door.

After an uncomfortable moment watching Jayne busying herself with dishes and trays, Hodge at last wandered from the Hall. He found refuge in the dovecote. The throaty murmurings of the doves and pigeons and the sweet smell of fresh-strewn straw helped to settle his feelings. Sitting in the shadows there, he forgot about Tom Dalby and chess games and luncheons with the prince.

Instead he thought of the chattering brook and wild birds on the wing, singing as they flitted through the trees. If only *he* were free to leave the castle. He remembered Prince Leo asking about the postern—the small sally port tucked away in a corner of the outer ward. Hodge wished he knew how to open it. If only it wasn't locked up tight. If only he knew who held the key.

A heavy rumbling interrupted his musings. He stood on tiptoe and peered through the slatted window of the dovecote. Wagons rolled over the planks of the drawbridge and through the gatehouse into the inner ward; wagons laden with provender—sacks of grain, barrels of malted ale, casks of new wine, great rounds of cheese, and gleaming blocks of salt. Normally such things were brought a cartload at a time, as need dictated. Today, however, twenty great wagons, pulled by broad-chested workhorses, trundled into the fortress, delivering supplies to last for what looked like a hundred score of days.

"What's this?" boomed Lord Selden.

Hodge ducked just as m'Lord stormed across the courtyard.

"What in *heaven's name* is all this?"

Hodge crept to the entrance of the cote.

Lord Selden stood at the first wagon, gesturing wildly at its driver. "We have no need of all these supplies!" he boomed. "This is not a hostelry."

The wagoneer climbed down and pulled a parchment from within his jerkin. "By order of the king." The rough man spat on the ground and handed the document to Lord Selden.

Findley and two other guardsmen appeared from within the Hall and strode up to the wagons. Hodge stole cautiously out into the ward, the better to see what was happening.

"M'Lord," Findley said, bowing slightly to Lord Selden. "We have been expecting these provisions. If you would kindly have your people unload the wagons."

"But where—"

Findley cut him off with a wave of his hand. "There is room in the pantries and the cellars. And what those won't hold can be stacked in the Hall and the garrison."

"But we have no need for so much—"

Again Findley interrupted him. "We have relied too much on your hospitality. The prince desires that such kindness be repaid."

Interrupting his own sputtering now, Lord Selden swelled out his chest. "Yes, well it has been our honor—"

Findley turned about and called to all who would hear. "Come! These provisions must be secured. Every able man, lend a hand."

Hodge was the first to step forward. "I'm here, sir!" he cried as he hurried to the nearest wagon. He hefted a bag of wheat onto his shoulders. "I can take another, if some-one will help."

A guardsman dropped another sack of grain on Hodge's back. "Now off ye go!"

Hodge staggered toward the kitchen, feeling almost invisible beneath his load.

"Let me help," called a voice. It was Fleet, just crossing from the mews.

"No," Hodge grunted. "Go get your own."

✦ ✦ ✦

It took the entire day to unload the wagons, even with every able-bodied man, woman, and child lending a hand. By the time they were done, the new supplies filled the pantries, overflowed the cellars beneath the keep, and heaped up to hide the east wall inside the Great Hall.

Hodge was tired and his feet hurt, but he stood back and appraised the piled sacks, barrels, and boxes with pride. He had worked hard all the day, right alongside the rest of the castle crew, so, though he was weary and sore, he was happy.

He twisted the stiffness out of his back and rubbed his hands on his legs. "Well, that's that!" he said.

"Yes, but what's it all for?"

Hodge looked up at Fleet, who had come to stand by his side.

"It's to pay us back," Hodge said. "I heard Findley say."

Fleet shook his head. "Pay us back for what?"

"Our hospitality."

"We haven't been *that* hospitable."

✦ ✦ ✦

That night, after the evening meal, the castle household gathered around the hearth in the Great Hall while Jesper told stories. The old man's long white hair and beard turned golden-red in the flickering glow of the fire. His eyes sparkled, and though his voice cracked with age, he still managed a pleasant timbre that held Hodge's interest at least as well as the tales themselves. Together the voice and words were hypnotic.

After the long day unloading wagons, Hodge was exhausted, but like the others he remained in the Hall and listened to every story. Old Jesper recited the tale of the Witches of Weston. He told of the giant at Allen-on-the-Lea. And, finally, he sang the lay of Prince William and the Siege of Nestor. It was at Nestor, uncounted ages ago, that Prince William the Cursed earned the name "Bloody Bill." For three years he held that old castle against invaders, surviving at the last by dining on enemy captives.

It was not a pleasant image to take to bed that night. Hodge said as much to Fleet as they retired.

"You're right, brother," Fleet said, "it's not. But I've heard other things that unsettle me more."

Hodge paused in laying out his blanket on the straw. "What things?"

"Oh, just rumors—from the wagoneers that came in today. Rumors about the prince." Fleet doused their torch in the bucket of water they kept at hand for the purpose. The tower room was cast into darkness. "And what about all those supplies? Oh, Jesper sees it, too. Why else would he tell the story of Bloody Bill? It's as if *we* were preparing for a siege."

"A siege?" Hodge asked. "From what enemy?"

"Those intent on rescuing the prince."

Hodge stopped with his mouth open. Fleet's words made no sense, bouncing around in his brain. They seemed backward, all scrambled up. "*Rescuing* the prince?" he finally blurted out. "From what? He's in no danger here."

"I believe he is a captive here. From what little bits I have heard from the wagoneers, it all makes sense: the guards, the provisions, even the prince bound to his room, stuck to using you for entertainment. For some reason, the prince is a prisoner."

"What? No!"

"What else could it be? I think the prince must have angered the king. Because of that, he has been brought here, under guard—the king's own guard—else he would be free to move about as he pleased."

"No! You are wrong! You listen to too many of Jesper's stories. Prince Leo is kind and good."

"Brother, calm down—"

"*You* calm down! I'm not the one talking crazy. You're just the falcon boy. You don't know anything."

"Hodge, I know what I see. I know what I've heard. The wagoneers talk of the king's displeasure with his son. They talk of trouble with factions. They talk of the hangings of other sons of noble birth. Your prince must be a danger to the kingdom."

Hodge was flabbergasted. "No. How can he be? He is teaching me to play chess."

Fleet sighed. "He is a prince. Why would he lower himself to associate with a common lackey?"

"You're jealous." Hodge rolled his blanket into a ball and hugged it to his chest. "You see me doing something besides shoveling muck, and it makes you jealous."

"Brother, no—"

Hodge turned and stalked from the tower. "I serve the prince," he said through gritted teeth. "And he accepts my service."

That night Hodge slept in the dovecote.

CHAPTER SEVEN

*D*espite the awful rumors that circulated through the castle, Hodge continued to serve meals to the prince. He scrupulously avoided Fleet, Lord Selden, and just about everyone else. He found himself lingering in the prince's chambers after each meal for as long as Findley would allow. First Findley would clear his throat. Then he would cough. Finally he would say, addressing the prince, "Your Highness, it is time you had your privacy."

Hodge carefully watched how Findley treated the prince. It was with notable deference, and not as a jailor.

"Fleet is crazy," Hodge told himself. "Prince Leo is no prisoner."

And then the prince would share with him the excitement of riding wild stallions across the northern steppes, and Hodge would feel a glowing happiness inside. Here was someone who desired his presence, who ignored his stooping back and wild eye.

With Prince Leo's help, Hodge was also improving at chess. He even won a game occasionally—of course with much "Uh, uh, uhing" on the prince's part. As Hodge came to understand the importance of each piece and its movement, the games became more interesting.

"It's like a battle!" Hodge finally exclaimed one rainy afternoon.

The prince laughed out loud at that. "Yes, a battle— though fairly safe for the combatants."

"Not for the Pawns. They're the first to go."

After a moment of quiet thought the prince said, "Yes. Often they are." He then showed Hodge how to better protect the Pawns by guarding them with more powerful pieces.

✦ ✦ ✦

Each night Hodge slept in the dovecote. Though he enjoyed the warbled cooing as the pigeons settled down to sleep, he missed wishing his tower owl "Good hunting." The dovecote had the advantage, however, in that Hodge could avoid Fleet's dreadful suppositions altogether. But he never could get all the feathers out of his tangled hair.

One evening as he and the prince played chess by the light of twenty candles, the prince pointed this out to him.

"Are you sprouting wings?"

"What?" Hodge glanced up from the chessboard. He had been trying to find a move to save his Knight.

In deference to Hodge's stature, they played at a low table so that Hodge could see the entire board and the position of each piece. Because of that, the prince had a good view of the top of his head.

"You've something in your hair," the prince said.

Hodge ran his fingers through his matted curls. A single white piece of fluff drifted to the chessboard.

"Feathers," he said, feeling a bit embarrassed. "Dove feathers."

"So, you are to become a fletcher after all."

Hodge was surprised that the prince would remember. "No, it's not—" Then he noticed the teasing grin. He smiled sheepishly. "No. I sleep in the dovecote."

"Ahhh. I can't imagine a pleasanter bedroom. There is nothing quite so relaxing as the moan of a dove. But perhaps you should comb out your hair when you arise in the morning. Then you wouldn't be trailing feathers all about."

"I have no comb." Hodge could feel the blush starting to turn his ears warm. He had never worried about such things before.

"You may have one of mine." The prince went to his dressing table and returned with a jewel-encrusted comb that sparkled in the candlelight. "This one should do nicely."

"But, I can't—"

"I insist." The prince knelt at Hodge's side and began combing out the tangles in his hair, as if he himself were Hodge's page.

The blush spread, burning through Hodge's face and into his scalp. "Your Highness, I—"

"Shhhh. Not another word. Or, if you will"—the prince lowered his voice—"tell me more about the caves you spoke of before. Those up in the wild hills."

"The caves?" Hodge whispered back. "Oh, they are wonderful. But you must take a torch. The tunnels go on forever. Chambers as grand as any palace. Columns and stairways and—"

"And how did you find them?" the prince interrupted.

His embarrassment quickly forgotten, Hodge now felt that he would burst with pride. "I discovered them myself while hiking through the hills. They're well hidden. I—I could take you there."

"No, there is no need. But . . . if I wanted to see them, what trail would I take?"

Hodge lowered his voice even further. The caves were his secret, shared with no one, not even Fleet. "Follow the

Eiderlee until you come to the falls. Not the little ones, but the big ones—the ones as grand as the veil of a queen. There is a deer trail along the slope, but take the opposite rise, straight up to the cliff face where you'll find a fallen rock near big as a wagon. Beyond that is the cave's doorway, just barely big as me."

Across the room, Findley cleared his throat.

The prince stood up and handed Hodge the comb. "Keep it. I insist." He lowered his voice again. "And perhaps one day you may find me in these caves of yours."

Once alone in the dovecote that night, Hodge held up his gift in the pale moonbeams that sifted through the slatted window. Though the moon was not yet to her full, and gathering clouds scudded across her face, the jeweled comb flashed and glimmered.

Hodge had never before touched such finery. He carefully laid the comb on the wooden ledge near where he made his bed. He sat down and pulled off his boots. He removed his belt. It was then he noticed his knife was gone.

✦ ✦ ✦

"Brother, what ho?"

Hodge ignored Fleet's call and hurried through the Hall, where he had been searching for his mislaid knife.

"Come now, Hodge. Don't be angry." Fleet caught him as he stepped out the doorway into the morning light. "Why do you flee me?"

Hodge said nothing, but stood squinting in the sun. It had rained during the night and puddles of water sparkled in the courtyard.

"Well?" asked Fleet.

"You know why."

"Because you are obstinate?"

Hodge grunted and started off across the courtyard.

"Wait," Fleet called. "I'm sorry." With his long stride he quickly caught up to Hodge. "Please, brother. Talk to me."

"Why should I? You'll only insult me again. Or tell me of some wicked plot or scorn my prince or—"

"Hodge. I will speak only the truth."

Hodge paused at the earnestness in Fleet's voice. "The truth?" he asked.

"Yes. No rumors. No guesses. Just the truth."

Hodge sighed. "All right. What is *the truth*?"

"The truth is, I fear for you."

"What? Again?"

"Yes, again. And still. I fear the prince is using you."

"Using me? Of course he is. I'm his servant."

Fleet shook his head. "No, Hodge. That's not what I meant. I fear he is using you for some sinister purpose. Otherwise his tolerance makes no sense."

"His tolerance?" Hodge shouted. "Why do you take pleasure in insulting me? The prince is my friend."

"And you are my brother!"

"That doesn't make you my lord!"

Hodge spun about and hurried across the ward. This time Fleet did not follow.

CHAPTER EIGHT

*T*hat night it rained again—a raging storm bolstered by great rolling cracks of thunder and blazing flashes that filled the dovecote with a white light. Hodge jumped at each searing boom. He never had been able to abide the devil's warring in the skies, so he huddled in his blanket with his knees drawn up, hoping each terrible crash would be the last. Though angry with Fleet, he wished they still shared the corner tower. He wished his brother had never said those things about Prince Leo. Then he wouldn't be spending the night alone in this awful storm. He pulled his head inside his blanket for protection.

In an effort to divert his mind from the chaotic tempest, he thought of the prince and their time together. He remembered the chess games. He imagined sharing the wonders of his cave with the prince—the limestone galleries, the glittering halls. No storm would ever penetrate there.

Hodge squeezed the jeweled comb in his hand and relaxed a bit. Though the rumbling thunder moved off in the distance, the rain continued, beating down on the roof of the dovecote, trickling through the thatch and dripping, *kerplunk*, to the floor. It made a pleasant kind of music that turned his mind from the battle just fought overhead. The night air had turned cool, so he burrowed with his blanket deeper into the straw. The steady drone of the rain made him drowsy. Soon he felt himself drifting toward sleep.

The trumpet's alarm startled him out of his dreams.

It was the call to assembly, something Hodge had never heard in the middle of the night. With his blanket still drawn over his shoulders, he crept to peer out between the dripping slats. The courtyard shimmered with the falling rain.

The prince's men-at-arms were the first to respond to the call. They gathered smartly in the courtyard before the Great Hall. Next came the castle's contingent of soldiers, grumbling at the nighttime summons. Finally, the tradesmen, cooks, butlers, pages, and various others slowly roused and wandered out into the rain, covered with blankets and sheepskins—though Bert the ostler stumbled out in just his nightshirt.

Hodge watched from inside the dovecote. He wondered what the commotion was about but did not relish tramping across the courtyard with the rain streaming over his back.

Several more guards appeared from within the Hall, torches held aloft. They barked orders, which sent the royal men-at-arms into immediate action. They fanned out across the courtyard and began a sweep of the entire keep. It appeared they were searching for something. They entered each outbuilding and shed, poking about with their torches and pikes.

It was only a matter of time before they would find Hodge huddled in the dovecote. He feared trouble for not responding to the trumpet, so he left his blanket lying in the middle of the dovecote and crept back beneath the roosts, where he wormed his way into the bird-soiled straw against the far wall. Lying as flat as possible, he tried to cover himself. The stench he stirred up made his eyes burn, but he didn't dare close them. So he peered out from beneath the filth, blinking against the sting.

A guard thrust a torch into the dovecote, upsetting the birds and sending them into a fit of flapping, fluttering noise. He quickly scanned the interior.

"If he was here," the guard called over his shoulder, "the birds would have let us know." He withdrew and moved on to search elsewhere.

Hodge let out the breath he had been holding, breathed in another, and gagged. He rolled away from the wall and jumped to his feet, sweeping the dirty straw from his face and clothes. He returned to his watch. The storm had begun to let up, but it was too late to save those who still stood in the dark courtyard. Hunched and shivering in their dripping blankets, they seemed nearly washed out by the streaming rain.

Hodge thought about what the guard had said. He wondered if someone had stolen into the castle. He couldn't imagine how, but the thought did not sit well in his mind. He peered back into the darkness of the dovecote. The birds were settling down. Perhaps the guard was right. If anyone unfamiliar came in here, the pigeons and doves would give sufficient warning.

The noise of the search continued, echoing about the keep. Hodge's legs grew tired from standing on his toes. At last the royal soldiers gathered back in the center of the court, and the people were dismissed to return to their interrupted sleep. Hodge saw Fleet pause to look about, as if he was searching for someone, too, but a guard pushed him away, shouting an order to move along. Fleet hurried to his corner tower.

Feeling a chill, Hodge returned to his blanket, but the squeal of the lowering drawbridge called him back. The gate opened and the royal guards were already quick-marching from the castle, save for a few who remained at the entrance to the Hall. From the stables rolled a cart pulled by one of the castle workhorses. The strange night was turning stranger still.

By the light of the flickering torches, Hodge saw something that made his heart drop within him. Two men shuffled from the Hall, carrying a third between them like a sack of grain. They lugged the body down the steps and carefully lifted it into the cart. From where Hodge stood, the body appeared to be a man's, but which man he couldn't tell. Was it Lord Selden? Jesper? Sir Granby? And then his stomach sank. Was it the prince?

The two men jumped into the cart and turned the horse toward the gate. Hodge found himself standing at the doorway of the dovecote beneath the breaking clouds, wishing he knew whose body was being carried from the castle.

✦ ✦ ✦

Hodge did not sleep the rest of the night. As soon as he sensed stirring in the kitchen, he pulled on his boots and ventured across the ward, splashing through the scattered puddles. The early morning courtyard seemed strangely empty at least from what it had been during the last few weeks. The soldiers had not returned from their nighttime excursion, and it appeared that no guard stood on the gate tower, nor at the gates themselves. Hoping to find some answers, he descended into the kitchen.

Bilda stood at the preparation table, looking cross and disheveled. She seemed wilted from last night's rain. "I'll not be baking today!" she snapped at poor Jayne Kemp, who had the misfortune of passing nearby.

The scullery maid appeared as frazzled as the cook. She offered a hesitant curtsy and then scurried away in confusion.

"Hard bread is good enough," Bilda muttered.

Hodge felt a reluctance to broach the subject of the night's events with her.

"There you are," called a voice from behind.

Hodge spun about just as his brother bounded down the steps into the kitchen.

"Where have you been?" Fleet demanded, grabbing Hodge by the shoulders.

Hodge twisted loose, impatient to ask his own questions. "What happened last night? What were they looking for?"

Fleet shook his head. "I thought it might be you. When I didn't see you . . ."

"I was asleep in the dovecote."

Fleet looked skeptical. "During the storm?"

"Yes. Until the trumpet disturbed me. I didn't want to get wet, so I stayed put."

"But the search? They didn't find you there?"

"What were they hunting for?"

"Hssst, you boys! Either make yourselves useful or find someplace else to gossip." Bilda stood threatening with a bread paddle clutched in both hands.

Hodge had felt it on his backside too often to want to suffer it today. He tramped up the kitchen steps and into the pale light. Wisps of smoke from morning fires hung lazily about the courtyard. A call echoed from the curtain wall. Chickens clucked and cackled.

"Well? What were they hunting for?" Hodge asked.

Fleet turned about and looked down into Hodge's face. "I'm glad to see you," he said. "I worried all night when you weren't there in the courtyard with the rest of us."

"I can take care of myself," Hodge answered.

Fleet arched an eyebrow. "Perhaps. But it seems there was someone loose in the castle."

"Who?"

"They didn't say. The guards searched the whole of the keep, but couldn't find a soul." Fleet smiled briefly. "Not even you."

"Was it someone dangerous?"

Fleet shrugged. "The guards searched with weapons drawn."

"Is the prince safe?" The image of a body being carried away stuck in Hodge's mind.

"There has been no word. I believe the intrusion may have been a rescue attempt."

Hodge scowled.

"You still don't believe me, do you?" Fleet turned to gaze at the sky above the crenellated walls. "Brother, what will it take to convince you?"

"When I serve the prince his breakfast, I will ask him."

✦ ✦ ✦

Though Hodge carried out his duty that morning, he felt ashamed of the meal he carried up the steps toward the solar: nothing more than dry bread and a bit of cheese, not at all fit for a prince. Bilda had grumbled something about damp sleep and aching joints as she thrust the tray into his hands. "This will do for His Highness," she had said.

Now Hodge crept up the steps, unsure of how he would be received with such a meager breakfast. The absence of watchmen at the foot of the stairs had unsettled him, but worse yet, the door to the solar remained unguarded and slightly ajar.

He walked hesitantly down the long hall and pushed through the entrance. A man stood at the table, leaning on his fists. He turned about at the squeak of the door. It was Lord Selden.

"Ah. You have brought us some breakfast." His voice was hoarse, as if a long night of booming had taken its toll. He rubbed his red-rimmed eyes and ran his hand through his hair. "Just leave it here," he said. "And bring us some wine."

Hodge glanced around the room. "Yes, m'Lord."

Sir Granby, the captain of the castle guard, stood at the far end of the table. Several royal guardsmen were also in the room. Two of them peered out the window across the courtyard. Findley was gone.

"Where . . ." began Hodge with a crack in his voice. He cleared his throat. "Where is His Majesty, the prince?"

Lord Selden placed a hand on Hodge's back and steered him toward the door. "Please, boy, bring us some wine. And some more bread. And we need some cleaning done. Send up a maid with a bucket of water."

"Yes, m'Lord."

Hodge stood in the hallway for a moment, confused and uncertain. Hesitantly, he turned toward the stairs, but Sir Granby's voice pulled him back.

"They threaten siege if we don't agree to their terms."

Hodge couldn't help but listen now.

"And what are their terms?" Lord Selden asked. He sounded tired.

"They demand that we surrender and return Prince Leo to them," said another. "They will let the garrison go free, including the men they captured last e'en. They simply want the traitor."

"That makes no sense," said Lord Selden. "Don't they

know the prince is not here? That he has escaped? Surely he has already joined them."

"Perhaps this is some scheme Leo has hatched," said the third voice. "An excuse to conquer the castle on the pretext of his own rescue."

"Ah," said Lord Selden. "That would put us in a tight spot."

"Or perhaps the prince is lost," said Sir Granby. "The moat is deep. The walls are steep. However he managed his escape, perhaps it has accomplished what the king could not bring himself to do."

"In which case," said Lord Selden, "we are truly lost."

At that Hodge fled, forgetting about the request for more bread and wine. Tears smarted in his eyes as he rushed down the stairs and across the Hall. He didn't stop until he burst into the mews where Fleet was raking up the straw.

"The prince is gone!" Hodge gasped. "I've got to find him."

CHAPTER NINE

By noon it had become obvious to the castle's inhabitants that they were under siege. Faster than a falcon's flight the news had spread throughout the household
until even the butcher's boy had heard of their peril. Only
guardsmen were now allowed to watch from the towers
and walls, but every other pair of eyes had already
scanned the sky for evidence of danger. Plumes of smoke
and circling crows rose from the plains, marking the be-
sieger's encampment. All movement within the courtyard
ceased, except for an occasional scurrying from the Hall to
the soldiers' garrison. It was as if they expected danger to
rain down upon them from above.

A silent panic lay just under the surface of all the business of the castle. In the kitchen Bilda's voice had turned
quiet and distracted. Even the pots and pans seemed

nervously muffled as they bubbled with the midday stew of beef and turnips.

Hodge stood just inside the kitchen door and peered out, one eye examining a flock of geese that flew in the hazy distance. With the other eye he watched the scattered guards on the towers and walls. They were few, and they kept themselves behind the merlons for protection from the enemy below. Hodge ached to climb up with them to see if he could spot the prince in the enemy's midst. But he had already been turned away twice.

He spied Fleet hurrying across the ward.

"Brother," Fleet said, ducking past Hodge and through the doorway, "I have found out some news."

Hodge shrugged. Though he seethed with anxiety inside, he tried to appear disinterested.

"Lord Selden did not know the prince was a prisoner until just last night," Fleet said. "Until after the escape. Sir Granby told me. It was kept a secret from all but the royal guard. And Martin's Mary said she had to clean blood from the floor of the solar. Someone was injured. The prince must have found a weapon."

Hodge shrugged again. He glanced down at his belt where his knife had been. A knot formed in his stomach.

"And," Fleet continued, "no one knows how the prince managed to leave the castle. Or why his armies stay and still demand his release."

Hodge shrugged one last time. "Perhaps . . . perhaps

they are not his armies. Perhaps they are here to do him harm."

"Not his armies? Whose would they be?"

"I don't know. But why else would the prince hide from them?"

Fleet shook his head. "More likely, as Sir Granby believes, he did not survive the escape."

"No! Don't say that. He did survive. And I know where to find him."

"Where?"

"I'll not be telling you. You hate the prince. You would give him away."

"I don't hate the prince. But Hodge, he is a traitor. A danger to our king and our country."

Patches of red flashed before Hodge's eyes. Before thought could stop him, he swung his fist and caught Fleet in the stomach, doubling him over with a sharp exhalation of air.

Fleet sprawled back against the wall, gasping as he struggled to catch his breath. "Bro—brother! Why?"

"Don't call me brother. I serve the prince. I will find him, and then you will see that he is no traitor!"

Despite his bent back, Hodge tried to stand tall as he stalked across the courtyard. "You will see," he said. "You will *all* see." To his relief, his words bolstered his own conviction. He refused to believe what it seemed he must.

✦ ✦ ✦

The matter was simple. Hodge but needed to follow the prince to find the answers. He waited until the evening twilight hung heavy about the castle towers, when torches guttered in the Hall and shadows melted into the spreading darkness. Under cover of dusk he crept into the outer ward and sneaked his way along the curtain wall, until he came to the postern.

Prince Leo had asked him about this sally port during one of their chess games. Hodge had improperly moved a Rook. The prince patiently corrected him. Then he explained that the Rook represented the stronghold of the King—a protection in time of danger. "But," he said, "even in a fortress there may be weaknesses." He went on to talk about posterns and towers and barbican gates.

Now Hodge wondered if this very sally port had been the means of the prince's escape. In the gloom he carefully examined the thick oak door, set deeply into the outer wall. The door was bound with iron and secured in place with heavy hinges, a thick bar, and a forbidding lock. Hodge swept away the cobwebs. Darkness was rapidly closing in on him, but even so, he could make out the rust that flaked from the metal fittings. He kicked his feet through the weeds that grew all around. It was plain; this door had not been opened for many years.

He slid to the ground and sat in the wild grass. He heard the hoot of an owl as it swept overhead. He strained to catch a glimpse of its darker shape flying against the sky. It was his tower owl. "Good hunting," he whispered. Then it was gone. If only he could fly, too.

And then he remembered a story Jesper had told many weeks ago as they sat around the roaring fireplace in the Great Hall, long before they had ever been touched by rumors of the prince or his arrival. It was the story of King Ermentrude and his impossible escape from the mountain fortress of le Chevalier de Mal Compris.

Hodge jumped up at the memory. "That's what I'll do!" He clapped a hand over his mouth, startled by his own voice. Afraid of discovery, he crept away from the postern. "That is what I'll do," he whispered, nodding his head.

The feathers would be easy to come by—the dovecote, the mews, and even the courtyard would yield a bountiful harvest of those. Pitch could be had from the apothecary. And for the supporting structure there was the wild yew that grew beneath the oriel windows of the chapel. All the necessary parts were there, available to him, if he were clever enough. He lay awake that night, fitting together the plan in his mind. The soft cooing of the doves provided a welcome assurance that it would all work. At last he fell asleep with Prince Leo's comb in his hand, and dreamed of soaring high through the clouds.

✦ ✦ ✦

Hodge was jolted awake at first light. In his sleep he had imagined the ground shuddering beneath him. He sat up, instantly alert. The pounding of his heart told him that something had happened. He rubbed his face. There was another thump and the ground shook again, nearly bouncing him out of his blanket. It was as if a giant had slammed its fist into the earth.

Strident shouts echoed about. Hodge threw off his blanket and hurried out into the misty dawn. It took him a moment to realize what was different about the courtyard. Two boulders that hadn't been there yesterday were embedded in the ground near the Hall.

A warning trumpet sounded from the high tower. Soldiers armed with crossbows scurried along the battlements. Then there was silence, except for a nervous clucking from the courtyard hens. Faces peered out anxiously from cote and Hall.

As if in echo to the tower trumpet, another horn sounded in the distance. A moment later Sir Granby rushed from the high tower and hurried across the courtyard to meet Lord Selden, who had just appeared wearing only his dressing robe and an anxious look. Lord Selden nodded at Sir Granby's whispered words, then the two proceeded toward the gates. A pair of the royal guardsmen joined them. Hodge followed, keeping to the side of the yard, his empty stomach knotted up with nervousness.

The gates opened upon the lowering drawbridge.

Hodge wished he had a better view of the outside, but he didn't dare stray too far from the safety of the wall. After a moment, a single man stalked boldly through the castle entrance, holding aloft the white flag of parlay. He stopped just inside the gates. Alone, Lord Selden advanced to meet him. They each bowed in turn. The visitor spoke first. Hodge couldn't make out what was said, but the meaning seemed clear when the man pointed at the boulders.

Lord Selden shook his head. His voice boomed loud enough to be heard even in the farthest corners of the keep. "The prince is not here."

The stranger was quiet for a moment. He looked past Lord Selden toward the Great Hall. His eyes rose to the towers and battlements around him. And then he cast his gaze about the inner ward, resting at last on Hodge's hobbled form. Hodge nearly sprang back at the malice in the man's look. "You lie!" he growled, anger carrying his voice around the courtyard.

Hodge shivered at the cruel face, so unlike Prince Leo's comfortable joviality. The two men were obviously worlds apart. Hodge knew then that he was right and Fleet was wrong: The besieging army was not here to rescue the prince but to destroy him.

"Three days," the man said, "and then we will smash your walls to pieces." He dropped the white flag, turned about, and strode from the castle, leaving Lord Selden to face the gatehouse alone. Sir Granby hastened to his side. They turned and walked quickly back to the Hall, the other guards hurrying along after them.

Hodge ran to the spot where the parlay had taken place. He stooped to retrieve the white flag. "Three days," he mumbled to himself. He must hurry, too, or he would never have time to carry out his plan.

CHAPTER TEN

*H*odge adjusted the bundle on his shoulder and placed a foot on the narrow step. He glanced furtively back across the dark outer ward. He had thought the feathers would be lighter, but he'd had to use so much pitch and twisted hemp to hold them all to the yew frame that the contraption had turned bulky and awkward. He shook his head. "It'll work," he murmured. "It'll work just fine."

He glanced up at the top of the wall. The crenellated battlement formed a dull outline against the starry sky. He began his climb. As late as it was, no guards would be looking toward the inside of the castle. They would be on the towers, watching the waning fires of the enemy encampment. So Hodge avoided the tower stairs and ascended the precariously narrow steps built into the outer wall itself.

There was barely room for him, his bundle, and the cool night air, so he inched upward a step at a time, clutching at the rough stonework with his hands.

He crouched at the top of the stairs and peered along the wall walk. A breeze swept through the crenels of the parapet, ruffling his hair. The walk appeared empty. No movement disturbed the darkness of the outer towers.

He crept onto the walkway and hunched down behind the battlements. Adjusting his bundle once again, he stood on tiptoe and peeked between the merlons. The parapet was too wide for him to see the ground below, but he could feel the breeze now blowing full in his face. It carried the woodland smell of moss and damp leaves.

He unwrapped his bundle. Pitch-coated feathers stuck to the blanket as he peeled it from his creation. He cursed silently and wiped his sticky hands on his jerkin. "It'll work," he reminded himself. He separated the two sections and set them within the crenel. Then with great effort he struggled up into the niche himself. The ground below opened to his view. He looked down at the rocky berm between the castle wall and the moat. He realized that one of two things would happen when he spread those wings and jumped out into the night air. Either he would soar like a bird into the sky, or he would drop like a stone.

But what choice did he have? Tomorrow was the third day. The enemy troops had been using a trebuchet to hurl reminders over the castle wall. Just this morning poor Martin's Mary had been killed by a small stone as she scurried from the well to the kitchen. And shortly before sunset, the body of a captured royal guard had dropped into the courtyard as if it had fallen from the sky. That grisly sight had strengthened Hodge's resolve and further convinced him that the besieging enemy had nothing to do with the prince.

He checked to ensure that the jeweled comb was still safely tucked under his belt. He wriggled his arms into the frames and turned to face the world. A breeze caught the wings, tugging them wide, sending tiny whirlwinds of feathers off into the night. He flexed his legs. Then he jumped.

PART II

Escape

Hope, follow as you may.

CHAPTER ELEVEN

*T*hough both his guesses proved wrong, Hodge hadn't long to dwell on his disappointment. He neither soared like a bird nor dropped like a rock. It was more like the spiraling fall of a winged maple seed at the mercy of the wind. He tried to flap his arms, but that only sent him reeling sideways. Unable to correct himself he plunged headfirst into the moat, disturbing its calm with a heavy splash.

A fall on the rocks would have been kinder, he thought as he struggled to regain the surface. He pushed the wings downward and burst into the night air, sputtering and gasping. He sank again and gagged on a mouthful of water. Another strained push and he was able to spew the muck from his mouth. He kicked his feet, as if running. He swept the wings outward and back, outward and back. Finally, jerking and bobbing with the effort, he managed to keep his head above water.

Calls from atop the castle wall gave him bearing. By twisting his body, he was able to maneuver across the moat.

Then he understood the cries.

"Halt!"

"Who is there?"

"We will shoot!"

Hodge tried to answer, but water rushed into his mouth. He could only gasp in a choked voice, "It's me!"

A quick *sploosh* sounded near him. Then another behind. Crossbow bolts zipped into the moat. Hodge increased the pedaling of his legs, but his left shoulder had stiffened, slowing his motion. He must have wrenched it in the fall. With his arms outstretched, the wings' buoyancy barely kept his nose above the water's surface.

The right wing jerked as a bolt pierced it through beneath his elbow. In a panic, he wriggled his arms free of the feathery targets. Without their support, he sank once again. Kicking frantically, his foot stuck in a gooey ooze. He pushed against it with all his strength and clawed at the dark water. He burst through the surface just long enough to suck in another breath. He sank again. He pushed at the muck. He breathed. Sank. Pushed. Breathed. Sank. Pushed. And hit his chin on the moat's far bank.

"I think I killed him," called a voice from the wall.

Clinging to the dank earth, Hodge looked back. The wings, shining almost white, slipped beneath the oily water. He gasped for breath and had to stifle a cough. Not daring to move, he waited for both the guardsmen's noise and the pounding of his own heart to subside, though it seemed the hammering in his chest would last forever. His shoulder ached, and his chin smarted. And he was chattering cold from the wet. Finally, he could bear it no longer. With his one good arm, he pulled himself up the bank and rolled into the weeds and grasses that edged the moat.

He hadn't long to rest. Other voices called from place to place in the fields around him.

"Over there!" shouted one. "A commotion from the castle walls."

"Be careful," called another. "It could be a trap."

Hodge pushed himself to his feet.

"There!" cried a third. "I heard something."

Hunched close to the ground, Hodge froze. The tasseled grasses tickled his nose. Water dribbled into his eyes. The night breeze whispered through his wet clothes, making him shiver all over again.

"Near the moat," called the first.

"Have a care."

"Shoot first."

Hodge shivered again, though this time it was not from

the cold. He could almost feel the shadowy forms creeping toward him in the darkness. In desperation he selected a spot somewhere between the last cries.

"Halt, there!" came a call from the castle wall behind him.

Voices seemed to be coming from everywhere to fill the night air. A twang sounded, then a groan and a heavy thud not ten yards to Hodge's left. He scuttled across the field. More shouts. Heavy footfalls. Cries of pain. He raced ahead, trying to outrun the commotion, his one thought to make it to the Eiderlee and then up into the hills. At any moment he expected to be tripped from behind. His heart pounded in his ears, his breath came in gasps, his side burned with the pumping of his legs. He thought he should have reached the stream by now. He could see the dark hills piling up like clouds in the night sky. He wondered why he couldn't hear the tumbling water. He stopped wondering when his foot stepped out into empty air. With a startled cry he pitched headlong down the rocky bank.

Out of nowhere, a vision of Fleet flashed through his mind. Then his head struck stone, and the world exploded into a million fragments of memory, a sliver of Fleet's face shining on each. The fragments flickered into darkness.

✦ ✦ ✦

When Hodge opened his eyes, there was no change from the blackness behind his lids. He panicked. A rushing sound filled his ears. It was a familiar noise that he could cling to, though not quite identify. Perhaps wind or rain or . . . water tumbling over rocks! He pushed himself to a sitting position and with difficulty steadied his wobbling frame. He winced at the pain in his head. He fingered the knot at the back of his skull, wondering how it came to be. And why his clothes were damp, and why he sat in the darkness with his feet in the stream.

Unbidden, the image of a chess piece—a Pawn—jolted into Hodge's awareness. All at once he recalled his purpose.

"Prince Leo!"

He clutched at his belt, trying to pull out the item he had carried there—the memento given him by the prince. But it was gone, lost somewhere between the Eiderlee and the castle wall. He had no desire to go back that way. He struggled to his feet, battling the dizziness that sent waves of nausea through him.

Though darkness still hung about in the valley of the stream, the faint light of dawn had crept into the eastern sky. The third day had arrived!

Bent nearly to the ground, Hodge crawled over rocks and through standing pools, gradually making his way along the churning water into the hills. His left shoulder pained him still, but he clenched his teeth and continued on. By the time he reached the lower falls, full daylight had crept its way through the woods. He sank to his knees and rested on the cool ground. His mind would not be still. He wished Fleet were here. But then he remembered with bitterness that Fleet did not like the prince.

"Then I can do this myself," Hodge whispered.

Steeling himself against the nausea, he labored up the rocky falls and on along the stream. When he reached the deer path at the second falls, however, exhaustion dragged him nearly to the ground. His head throbbed. Spots of color swam through his vision. Blinking hard, he gazed past the stream and up the hillside toward the hidden cave. He needed rest, but there was no time—the third day was slipping away.

Leaving the deer path behind, he slithered into the water. Its icy cold made his breath catch. He struggled through the waist-deep stream only to collapse on the far bank. He closed his eyes to try and steady the spinning of his head, but that made the whole world roll about him. He clenched his fists in the moss and ferns, hanging on for his life. Finally the nausea found release.

Once the brook had washed away all trace of his sickness, he lay on his side with his cheek resting amongst the ferns and let exhaustion have its way. He lay there only a short while, however, before the *chip, chip, chip,* of an invisible bird reminded him that time was passing. He groaned, flexed his aching shoulder, and pushed himself to his feet.

With barely an upward glance he climbed toward the boulder that hid the entrance to his cave. He knew in his heart the prince would be waiting there. He had to be.

Hodge hauled himself up the slope and at last reached the sheer cliff face that rose in crags and scrubby pine another hundred feet above him. The nausea returned. After a moment of empty retching, he leaned against the boulder, panting to catch his breath. Then he ducked behind the giant stone and stepped into cool darkness.

"Hello," he called. "It's me, Hodge. Hello."

His voice reverberated down the long corridors.

"Your Highness, I'm here."

There was no answer but his echo and the constant breeze that whispered up from the depths of the earth. He took a step forward, wary of the slanting fall to his right where a steep incline ended at a rocky wall. He couldn't see it in the inky blackness, though he knew it was there. He cursed himself for not bringing a torch, but then realized it would have been as wet as he was.

"Hello!"

Still nothing. He slumped down on the narrow ledge. Fear and disappointment battled within him: fear that Sir Granby was right—that the prince had not survived his escape; and disappointment that he *had* survived, yet had not come here. Hodge let out an exhausted breath that shook his whole body.

At first he thought the groan he heard was an echo of

his own. He kept still and listened, but could hear only the wind. He rose to his knees, his ears straining. There it was again! An unmistakable moaning.

He crawled forward, keeping to the shelf that led deeper into the cave, toward the first gallery.

"Hello," he repeated—softly, so the echoes would not veil a reply.

"Here," whispered a voice from his right, from the darkness at the bottom of the fall.

"Your Highness!"

Carefully he tried to ease himself down the slope. The smooth rock gave little purchase, but with effort he managed to lower himself bit by bit. But then he lost his grip and slid down the last five feet, scraping his chest and landing in a heap.

Without bothering to check his injuries, he struggled to his feet. "Where are you?"

"Hodge?"

"Yes, Your Highness."

"I've fallen. I fear I've broken my leg."

The prince's voice was weak and uneven. Hodge followed the sound of it, reduced to feeling his way in the darkness.

"I knew you'd be here," he said.

"I knew you'd come." Prince Leo's voice sounded heavy with relief.

Hodge stumbled against something soft. "Is that you?"

"Be careful. My leg."

"Are you hurt bad? I can't see."

The prince groaned in answer. "Badly enough," he said. "And I've run out of water." Then he coughed, though it might have been a feeble laugh. "Why didn't you tell me the cave was not for someone of my stature?"

"What?"

"I fair conked my head coming in. That's why I fell. That's why my leg is broken."

"I'll . . . I'll get you out of here."

"First," the prince rasped, "something to drink."

"But I didn't bring—"

"I've a water skin. Fetch me a drink from the stream."

Hodge felt something being pressed into his hands.

"Yes, Your Highness."

"And my flint and steel. Bring us some light."

"Yes, Your Highness."

"And hurry."

Hodge groped his way back to the slope, but after several sliding attempts he realized with a sinking feeling that going up would be much more difficult than coming down had been.

CHAPTER TWELVE

*P*lease hurry," the prince whispered. "My throat is like
to close up with thirst."

"I'm trying." Hodge clawed at the rock, digging his fingers into whatever crevice or cranny there might be, but
his deformity made it impossible to get the leverage he
needed. He gasped as he slid back down.

"What's wrong?" the prince asked from the darkness.
"Are you all right?"

"I can't climb back up."

The prince snorted. "What a bright idiot you are. Well,
at least we can die together."

Hodge clutched the scrape on his elbow. "I'll find a
way." He began searching back toward the cave entrance.
He strained to part the darkness with his eyes. A trick of

his vision set the inky blackness swimming before him. He could feel the slope steepening, forming a sheer wall. With gritted teeth he followed, groping his way blindly. He stumbled over rocks and nearly fell.

"Did you find a way?"

Hodge jumped at the voice. He hadn't noticed the wall curving around and leading him right back to where he started.

"Not yet," he said. "I'll keep looking." But the opposite direction proved no better. Deeper into the cave, the slope also became an upright wall. Hodge's disappointment turned into despair. Perhaps the prince was right. They would die here together. But then he stumbled onto something that made his heart leap: a narrow cleft in the wall. A chimney of sorts. With his crooked back, Hodge had always been well suited to chimney climbing. Last spring, Bilda had sent him up the flue of the great oven to pull out a bird's nest. Finding the wee chicks charred from the first blaze since Christmas had broken his heart. He cradled them in his hands and carried them out to a far meadow, where he buried them beneath the larkspur and speedwell, ashamed that he had enjoyed the roast oxen of the feast the day before.

Now, with the dark still about him, Hodge sat with his back wedged against one side of the crevice and his feet braced on the other. And then he walked upward, carefully placing one foot before the other and pushing with his hands and elbows. He held his breath, growing more nervous with each step. He feared that the crevice would end before he arrived at the top—or that his strength would give out and the nausea return—or that something might reach out of the darkness and snatch his hammering heart away. Finally, however, he rolled onto the ledge that led to daylight. He nearly laughed with relief.

"I made it!" he called to the prince.

The answer was too faint to understand. It could have been "at last" . . . or simply a feeble gasp.

"I'll bring you water!" Hodge cried.

✦ ✦ ✦

After Hodge's successful climb, his resolution returned in full strength. He shook the giddiness from his head and the exhaustion from his bones and turned his attention to saving Prince Leo. Coming and going became a simple matter of sliding down the slope and then "walking" up the chimney again. Hodge made several trips bringing water, firewood, and kindling. The water he carried in Prince Leo's flask. The wood he tossed down the slope, careful to avoid the prince. The kindling he stuffed into his jerkin and then slid down himself.

He struck spark to tinder, and soon a roaring blaze sent shadows dancing across the rock walls. A breath of air from the deep caverns pulled the smoke up to slip out the hidden entrance to the cave.

In the flickering light the prince's face seemed pale and drawn. "Lord Hodge," he said. "You have saved me. I thank you."

"Not yet I haven't. I'll need help getting you out of here. Perhaps I should go back to the castle. I can fetch Lord Selden—"

"No, that won't be necessary."

"But I can't care for you alone."

"Just bring me food." Prince Leo shook the bag he had carried from the castle. "All I've left is crumbs."

"You must come back. To prove yourself." Hodge searched the darkness for the right words. "They've said you are a traitor to the king. You must come back to save the castle."

Prince Leo only stared into the crumbling embers beneath the flames. The coals seemed to be alive with the red glow that ebbed and flowed across their surface. Hodge could do nothing but echo the prince's silence.

"My father is a fool," Prince Leo said at last. "He is a weak old man who has wasted everything I ever cared for. I hate him."

Hodge was stunned by the fierce invective in the prince's voice. "But—but what about the castle? Lord Selden? Bilda? My brother, Fleet?"

"What about them?"

"They are under siege. The enemy threatens to batter down the walls. I fear what will happen then."

"A siege! This is news indeed. What army is it?"

"An evil army. I fear they have come for you."

The prince's manner became more animated, as if this news excited him. "What banners do they bear?"

"I couldn't tell in the dark."

"You must go and find out, then return to me. And bring food. Bread and cheese will do. And whatever meat you may find. And wine if you can manage."

"Yes, Your Highness. If I can."

✦ ✦ ✦

As Hodge toiled down the valley under the afternoon sun, the exhaustion returned. The warmth on his back, his aching muscles, the burning of his eyes all conspired against him. He tried to remember the last time he had slept, but his mind grew fuzzy. The murmuring of the brook pulled at him. He eased himself to the ground and leaned against a moss-flecked boulder.

"I'll rest just a moment," he said. Though the prince was too far away to hear, Hodge felt a need to explain. "Just until my head quits hurting."

He closed his eyes. When he opened them the valley was filled with evening shadows.

"Oh, you idiot!" He jumped to his feet. "You stupid idiot!"

He had slept the afternoon away. The prince would be distraught, waiting for his return. Hodge debated whether he should continue on his errand or go back and explain what had happened. But the food bag, slung over his shoulder, remained empty.

"I'll hurry," he said.

He sped along the stream, racing the coming night. Soon he was out of the woods and gazing across the open plain below. The castle stood like a sentinel in the distance. Enemy banners scattered the field, flapping in the stiff evening breeze, their silver and green gilded with sunset. The flags were too far off to make out their emblem, but Hodge had no desire to get any closer to the enemy camp. Reporting their colors would have to be enough. He turned his attention to the next task the prince had set for him: finding food. The inhabitants of the village had always been happy to share their bread with him. If he was careful and kept within the banks of the brook, he could sneak around the field and enter the town undetected by enemy soldiers. There, he would find welcome.

Stealth, however, proved more difficult than he had expected. Every unidentified noise set him on edge, every wisp of breeze sent shivers of panic down his spine. Several times he threw himself to the ground thinking he was discovered, only to find it was his own imagination stalking him. By the time he crept beneath the willow at the edge of the village his boots were sloshing wet, his leggings soaked to his thighs, and his nerves rattled almost beyond repair.

He breathed a little easier amongst the houses and shops that clustered around the ancient church, but he wondered at the absence of light in the windows. Evening had already cast its velvet across the sky, and Hodge had to squint to pierce the gloom. He crept through the silence, approaching the door of Tolman the tanner. He rapped softly. There was no answer. He eased the door open.

"Hello?"

Darkness filled the single-room hut. No blaze glowed upon the hearth, no candles sputtered. No evening meal sat steaming on the table, and no children squealed with delight at seeing Hodge at the door.

"Maggie? Brand? Hod Tolman?"

The rustling of rats in the roofing thatch was the only answer. Hodge backed out of the house and hurried to the home of Red Robert the cooper. It too was empty. So was the next. And the next. Even the church was deserted. The town had been abandoned.

Hodge stood at the last house and gazed at the fires of the enemy camp. Where were the villagers? What could have happened to them? He shook the apprehension from his head. At least there would be food here. At least he could gather dinner for the prince. He turned to retrace his steps.

"You!" shouted a voice from near the willow tree. "Stop!"

Hodge heard the jangle of a horse's bridle. He spun about the other way, but a dark shape jumped out of the shadows and knocked him to the ground. Light flashed into his face as a lantern was uncovered.

"A spy," hissed the figure. "A stinkin' spy."

CHAPTER THIRTEEN

*H*odge blinked at the light, trying to see into the darkness beyond.

A voice growled, "Why, it's nothin' but a boy."

Horses' hooves clattered to a stop, followed by the squeak of leather and the heavy tread of boots.

"Just a boy? What kind of boy?"

"Get up," commanded the first. "Come on! Get up."

Hodge hauled himself to his feet.

"Stand up straight!"

"I . . . I am," Hodge stammered.

The lantern man thumped him on the head, nearly knocking him down again. "I said stand up straight!"

Hodge whimpered at the pain. "I am. My . . . my back won't—"

Then the horseman grabbed him by the chin and pulled his face up into the light.

"Pah. It *is* just a boy."

"He could still be a spy," said the other.

"A spy, eh? Now here's a chance."

"Yeah, a spy. Kill him and let's get on."

"You're an ass. If he's a spy then he knows as much of the king's army as he does of ours. He'd be worth something."

"Then *you* can be the one to take him into camp. It's all the same to me."

"Ah, that's a sticky matter," said the horseman. "Bothering Lord Pertwie without good cause can be . . . sticky."

"Then kill the brat!"

The horseman held Hodge tight. "Well, boy. Are you a spy?"

Hodge tried to shake his head, stuttering out his answer. "N-No. I'm Hodge. I'm no spy."

"Then what are you doing here, sneaking around in the dark?" He gave Hodge's chin a fierce squeeze.

"Nothing!"

"Nothing?" He squeezed again.

Hodge thought his jaw would crack. "Just looking for some food."

"Ah, a thief," said the lantern man. "A scavenger." He glanced at his companion. "The brat's a rascal, hoping to make his fortune off the dead."

"Or still a spy," growled the other. "I judge I'll take a chance on Pertwie's anger. Better to bother him over nothing than let this rascal report our strength to the king."

The man looped a long leather strip over Hodge's hands and drew it tight. Then, holding fast the other end, he leaped onto his horse.

"Come along, boy," he said.

The leather pulled tight, nearly jerking Hodge off his feet. His legs flailed as he struggled to keep up with the trotting horse. He stared at the rushing ground, watchful for rocks that could send him stumbling to his face.

Soon flickers of yellow light flashed by on either side, but Hodge didn't dare raise his head. Snatches of noise rushed past: clangings and thumpings and rough voices. Without warning the horse stopped and Hodge tumbled to the earth. He craned his neck to see. A silver and green banner floated above him in the firelight.

"An oak leaf!" Hodge cried, recognizing the emblem.

A violent yank jerked him to his feet.

"Come on," shouted the horseman. He pulled Hodge within a blaze of torches.

Though the world spun in confusion around him, Hodge had the impression of men standing, talking, arguing—then turning quiet as he became the center of attention.

"M'Lord Pertwie," the horseman said, bowing.

Hodge gasped. He recognized the nobleman sitting at

the long table, lit by the glow from countless braziers and torches. It was the man who had carried the white flag of parlay into the castle but three days ago.

"Yes?" Lord Pertwie said, drawing out the question as if it were more important than any answer.

"M'Lord, I've caught a spy. In the village."

"A spy? Let me see him."

The horseman pulled Hodge forward.

"Make him stand up straight." Lord Pertwie pointed at Hodge with a half-eaten chicken leg.

A kick from behind sent Hodge stumbling forward. He nearly crashed into the table.

"You heard m'Lord."

Hodge kept his head lowered, fearful that Lord Pertwie would recognize him. "I can't stand straight," he said. "I was made this way. I can't help it."

Lord Pertwie's cold stare turned upon the horseman.

"A spy, you say."

"Yes, m'Lord." There seemed to be a hint of doubt in the horseman's voice.

"And where did you say you found this wicked spy?"

"In yonder village."

Lord Pertwie glanced to the guards on either end of the table. "Stand him up straight," he said, pointing again with the greasy bone.

With one on each side, the guards grabbed Hodge by

the shoulders and pulled, as if they intended to break him in two. He cried out in pain.

"He won't bend," said one of the guards at last.

They dropped him to the ground.

"A spy," said Lord Pertwie again. "You are so clever to have caught a spy. And so clever to have brought him straightway to interrupt my supper." In an explosion of rage he hurled the bone at the horseman. "You have brought me a cripple! Nothing but a useless peasant! You are an idiot. Go, get out of my sight."

With a hurried bow, the horseman turned and disappeared into the crowd of soldiers that stood watching.

Then, to Hodge's surprise, Lord Pertwie burst out laughing. "This misshapen boy, a spy! Look at him. Not worth the boots on his feet."

Others joined in Lord Pertwie's laughter.

In shame, Hodge arose. He tugged the leather strap from his hands. Then, with the voices echoing in his ears, he turned and ran, pushing his way through the soldiers who swatted at him as he passed.

✦ ✦ ✦

Nearly numb with exhaustion and fatigue, Hodge stumbled at last into the cave. The fire had long since burned out.

"Your Highness," he called. "I've returned."

Unable to control his slide, he hurtled down the incline into absolute darkness. He lay still for a moment, letting the effort of breathing take all his attention. The darkness seemed less intense with his eyes closed.

"Did you bring wine?" asked the prince, startling Hodge out of the silence.

Hodge staggered to his feet. "No, Your Highness. But I've brought more water. And bread and cheese. And an onion. I found them in the village, on my way back." At least he had done that much.

"What took you so long? I expected your return hours ago. You worried me."

Hodge hung his head. "I . . . I fell asleep on the way. I'm sorry. I couldn't help it."

"You fell asleep?"

"And I was captured. But I escaped."

"Captured? By whom?"

"By the enemy. I've seen their colors."

"And?"

"Silver and green. Their banners are silver and green. A silver oak leaf on a green field."

"Ah," said Prince Leo. "Lord Pertwie."

Hodge nodded, though in the darkness the prince would never see it. "Your Highness, he is a wicked man."

"That he is," said the prince.

CHAPTER FOURTEEN

"Go to sleep now," commanded Prince Leo. "There's much to do tomorrow. And I'd prefer you not nap in the middle of it."

The words made Hodge wince with shame. "Yes, Your Highness."

He hunched down against a rock and pulled his arms within his jerkin. Though a summer's night lay heavily upon the forested slopes without, wisps of cold air moved about the cave, drifting from the damp places below. Too tired to fetch wood to start a fire—too worn out even to strike flint to steel—Hodge huddled to himself and depended on the warmth of his own body to see him through the night.

In spite of the chill, exhaustion took its toll. Hodge

slept like one of the rocks that formed his bed, dreaming only once of his brother. In the dream Fleet shouted at him from just beyond the edge of hearing. Hodge waved his hand at his brother's noise and sank further into slumber.

When he finally awoke, it was impossible to tell daylight from black night. He craned his neck toward the entrance of the cave. A blush touched the darkness there.

"Your Highness," he whispered, unsure if the prince had awakened yet. "I think it's morning."

"Long into it," said the prince. "But you were snoring away so soundly it would have taken a trumpet to waken you. I've eaten all the cheese. But there is still plenty of bread if you like. You'll have to fetch water again. Then bring more light and I'll give you instructions."

Hodge felt better after the sleep. His head still ached a bit, but his stomach had settled considerably. Yesterday's exertion and last night's cold slumber on hard ground made his joints ache—yet the rest had done him good. Oddly, even the soreness of his shoulder seemed alleviated by all the other discomforts he felt.

He scooted up the chimney and scrambled from the cave. The midmorning warmth felt pleasant on his face. He sniffed the air. The faint odor of wood smoke drifted up the valley—doubtless the distant cook fires of castle and camp.

Fire for the prince, however, was not so easily kindled. First the tinder Hodge gathered was too damp from the morning dew, and the tiny blaze wouldn't catch hold. On the second attempt, Hodge stumbled as he tried to fan the flames and smothered them beneath his body. The third try, however, proved successful, and soon the fire-light danced across Prince Leo's face.

"Thank you," the prince said. "And now I have a task for you."

Hodge sat close, leaning forward into the flickering light, pleased to have a duty to perform.

Prince Leo pulled a golden chain from around his neck. A small object hung from the chain, glinting in the blaze. "This is my seal. Take it." He handed the chain to Hodge. "Give it to Lord Pertwie. Tell him where I am, and that I am injured."

Hodge nodded, his eyes fixed on the object. "Lord Pert—" He stumbled over the name. "You . . . you mean Lord Selden, don't you?"

"I know who I mean. Tell Lord Pertwie that I escaped from the castle through the privy shaft, that my father's man, Lord Findley, is dead, and that my leg is broken. Tell him he must come quickly. Tell him to bring ten men, a lit-ter, and rope."

Hodge stammered in protest. "L-Lord Pertwie? But he is—"

"You have sworn to serve me," interrupted the prince. "Now go!"

As Hodge stared across the plain at the enemy banners, Fleet's words came back to him. "I fear the prince is using you."

Hodge had been strong and sure in Prince Leo's defense, but now his confidence wavered. "There has to be a reason," he whispered to himself, though he couldn't imagine what it might be. "The prince is not a traitor!" He could not bring himself to believe it, and yet . . .

He let his gaze wander from the bristling banners of the enemy camp toward his castle home. A smoky haze hung about the towers. Blackened timbers stuck up at odd angles from the gatehouse roof. The curtain wall sagged in places. He watched in horror as a huge stone soared through the air and silently smashed into the wall, raising a cloud of dust and debris. Moments later a thundering crash reached his ears, coming, as it seemed, from another world.

In shocked disbelief he searched the field between the castle and the camp. A giant mangonel lurched, springing forward on its wheels. Its long arm catapulted a second stone toward the castle walls. Hodge covered his eyes, but he couldn't silence the rolling boom that followed. The third day had passed.

"Fleet!" he cried. All doubt disappeared. Clasping

Prince Leo's seal in his hand, he leaped into action. "I'll give you the prince," he said through gritted teeth, "only let my brother be!"

This time he made no attempt at stealth. With Fleet's danger bearing down on him, he rushed headlong across the wide field, though it seemed to take an eternity to cover the distance. After many minutes he at last ran huffing and puffing into the camp. There he spied a lackey, just emerging from a tent.

"You," Hodge called, darting forward. "I must speak with your master."

The man kicked at him. "Be off! There's no scraps to be had here today."

Hodge avoided the booted foot and continued through the rows of tents and beyond. He passed among the ranks of soldiers who seemed distracted by more important proceedings. Invisibility could not have given him better protection. Soon he spied a group of Lord Pertwie's knights who stood in advance of their army. Lord Pertwie himself faced a lone soldier who clutched a scrap of white cloth. It was Sir Granby, looking as slumped and defeated as the castle.

"So you have realized the impossibility of your situation?" Lord Pertwie said. "That is good. But you still have not brought Prince Leo to me."

Sir Granby slumped even further. "We cannot give him

to you," he said, "because we do not have him. He escaped four days—"

Lord Pertwie's slap made Sir Granby's head snap back. Sir Granby wiped the blood from his mouth with the back of his hand.

Lord Pertwie snarled. "You are stalling. You have hopes that King Alfred and his armies will rescue you. I can assure you that will not happen. By the time they arrive, the stones of Castle Marlby will be strewn about the countryside. All but those of the highest tower. From that I will hang you!"

Sir Granby spat more blood from his mouth. "That may be, but we do *not* have the prince. And if we did, we would not surrender him to you. Yours will be the only hanging from the tower."

Lord Pertwie raised his hand to strike again, this time with his fist clenched.

Hodge didn't wait for the blow to fall. "I can give you the prince," he cried, holding aloft the golden chain.

All heads turned.

Though shaking inside, Hodge hurried forward.

"Who is this?" said Lord Pertwie. "Do I know—wait, the crippled spy!" His mouth turned up in an unpleasant smile.

"What Sir Granby says is true," Hodge said. "Prince Leo has escaped. This is his seal. He is injured. I can take you to him."

Lord Pertwie snatched the chain from Hodge's grasp. He examined the seal. "How did you get this?"

"Prince Leo gave it to me."

"You're a scavenger, eh? You found a dead body and relieved it of its valuables."

"No! I told you. Prince Leo gave it to me. He commanded me to—"

"Kill the boy," Lord Pertwie said.

A soldier approached, sliding his sword from its sheath.

"No!" cried Sir Granby.

Hodge looked about for escape, but there was none. "Prince Leo is alive!" he shouted. "I can take you to him. You can see for yourself. How else would I have his seal?" He ducked his head at the raised sword.

"A moment," Lord Pertwie said. He bit his thumbnail in thought. "Perhaps the boy is telling the truth. Go with him. Find out."

Hodge almost fell to the ground in relief. "We must bring some rope," he said. "And a lantern. The prince is badly hurt."

Lord Pertwie signaled to the swordsman. The two spoke together for a moment in hushed voices. Then Lord Pertwie turned to Hodge. "You'll have your rope and a lantern."

"And the ten men?"

"There will be time enough for that later, when Hubert here is satisfied."

The soldier slid his sword back into its sheath. The rasping sound of metal on leather made Hodge shiver.

✦ ✦ ✦

Hodge pointed across the stream toward the hidden entrance to the cave. "Up there," he said to the soldier. "You can see our smoke from behind the boulder."

"Aye," said the man. "Let's get on with it."

Hodge plunged into the stream with the soldier following close behind. Hodge scrambled up the hillside. The soldier stayed right on his heels. At the mouth to the cave, Hodge warned him of the low ceiling and the drop to the right.

"That's how the prince fell," he said.

"Aye," was the only response. The soldier paused to light the lantern.

"Your Highness," Hodge called. "I'm back. We've brought a rope." He could see Prince Leo, sitting beyond the low fire, alight himself with anticipation.

"Good!" the prince said. "Is Lord Pertwie there?"

"No. Just me and one other. Lord Pertwie didn't—"

"Aye, that's the prince," said the soldier as he stooped under the stone ceiling. "I'll see to him." He set down the lantern and searched for a place to anchor the rope.

"Where is Lord Pertwie?" Prince Leo asked.

The soldier only grunted.

Once the rope was secured to a rocky outcropping, the man lowered himself toward the prince, taking the lantern with him.

"It'd be easier without that sword clanking at your side," Hodge called. He turned to climb down the rope himself. His heart froze at the slither of metal on leather.

"What's this?" cried Prince Leo.

Hodge swiveled about. The soldier formed a dark silhouette against the lantern light. Hodge saw a sword flash. He shoved against the slope with all his might, hurling himself at the man's shadow. He crashed into the soldier's back with a jarring crack.

Time stopped, gathered up in a single heartbeat as Hodge tumbled into darkness. No sparkling shards of memory relieved the emptiness this time. No visions of Fleet. No visions at all.

CHAPTER FIFTEEN

Shaking, shaking, shaking, as if on an early morning with Fleet trying to rouse him from deep slumber—a wintry morning of bitter, biting cold. Loath he was to stir from the comfort of blanket and bedding.

"Let me be," he groaned. "Let me sleep."

More shaking. And a whispering voice. And a smell of dank wood, or rock, or mossy water.

"Wake up, boy. Wake up." The voice was insistent.

"Brother, go away."

"I am not your brother. I am your prince. I command you to wake!"

A splash on his face. A sputtering cough. Stabs of light that split his head. Eyes peering into his.

"Am I . . . am I dead?"

"No, of course not."

"Are you?"

"No! But the assassin is."

Awakening then. And remembrance.

"Your Highness!" Hodge pushed himself to a sitting position. "What happened?"

The lantern lay on the rocky floor, its tallow candle miraculously still lit. It cast weird, elongated shadows on the roof of the cave. The prince had pulled himself to Hodge's side, past the wood fire that had been all but extinguished by the motionless form that lay across it.

"You brought a man to kill me," the prince said.

Hodge tried to shake off the wooziness that once again spun through his head. "No, I didn't," he said, rushing the words out between gyrations. "I remember. I took the seal as you commanded. I asked for help. Lord Pertwie sent only one man. No others. No litter to lift you out. Only rope and the lantern. I—"

"Pertwie sent the assassin?" interrupted the prince.

"What? No. I don't know. I asked for help, but—"

"Does Pertwie have my seal?"

Hodge wrestled with his memory, trying to place the chain and its whereabouts. "I think so."

"How could he?"

"I—I gave it to him, like you told me."

"No. How could he have done this? Pertwie is *my*

man." Prince Leo spat out the words as if they were distasteful to him.

Hodge lifted himself on unsteady legs. He nearly stumbled over the body. "Who is that?"

"The man you brought."

"What happened? How did he—"

"You must have broken his neck. Like a crossbow bolt you were, flying through the air, straight at him."

Hodge stepped away from the body. "Me? Straight? I'll never be straight."

"Perhaps. But once again you've come to my rescue. I understand what is happening now. Pertwie has betrayed me. The traitor! He deserves to die."

Hodge's struggle with himself was brief. At last he accepted what had been nagging at him for so long. "Lord Pertwie is *your* man. That makes *you* a traitor to the king."

The prince reached for the lantern. Upright it cast a more natural light. "My father is a weak and ineffective ruler," he said. "He has not the power to do what is best for his kingdom or his subjects."

Surprised at his own audacity, Hodge opened his mouth to say, "But you do?" only to have the words replaced with a sudden flash of insight. "And Lord Pertwie does?"

"No, not Lord Pertwie . . ." The prince stiffened. "Yes. I take your meaning. Pertwie has my seal. He commands my army. This assassin was sent to kill me, and only he and

Pertwie would have known. But for you they would have succeeded. And they still might." He pressed his fists against his forehead. "My plans, all ruined because of a blind fall in the dark."

"You must stop them."

"How? Now that I know Pertwie's intentions, I must stay here. You must take care of me. Bring me food and water. My leg is healing, I can feel it. I will not let Pertwie kill me. Then when the time is right—"

That was more than Hodge could bear. "But Fleet may be dying!"

"Brothers have died before. Yours won't be the first."

Hodge had never felt such a black rage. He sputtered as he tried to speak. His whole body trembled. Even in the bright lantern light a shadow seemed to have been cast over his vision.

"Hodge, are you all right?"

"You . . . you would kill my brother?"

Prince Leo's shoulders slumped, his hands dropped to his sides as if he had suddenly lost all his will. "No. Not I. But I've not the power to stop it."

Even through his anger, Hodge could feel the sadness in the prince's voice.

"You've saved me twice," Prince Leo continued. "I can ask no more. Go, find a way to rescue your brother. I cannot."

"But you're the prince. You're the one Lord Pertwie wants. If you can't—"

"I've not the power!"

Hodge's anger could not stand against Prince Leo's anguished cry. It struck him through the heart.

The prince turned his head. "Go," he said. "But before you leave at least take me away from this dead man. Get me to the stream where I'll have water. At least do this."

After a moment's hesitation, Hodge picked up the provender bag. "I'll try," he said. "But then I must go."

✦ ✦ ✦

In the end, Hodge had to tie the assassin's rope around Prince Leo's waist to haul him, bouncing and scraping, up out of the pit. Negotiating the hillside toward the stream proved to be even more difficult. The prince used Hodge as a crutch while they slithered and slid down the slope. Halfway to the stream, Hodge tried to stop to catch his breath, but his legs got tangled up with the prince's.

"Watch out!" he cried.

Before he could regain his balance, his feet slipped from under him, and the two tumbled down the dusty hillside, arms and legs flailing. A gorse bush finally stopped their descent.

Hodge jumped out of the prickles. "Your Highness, are you all right?"

Prince Leo groaned. His breathing came shallow and

fast, as if he were trying to speed himself through the pain. "Y-yes." He clinched his eyes closed. "No!"

"What should I do?"

"Get me out of this bush!"

Hodge helped the prince struggle to his feet. They wobbled awkwardly, trying to balance on the slope.

"Let's get off this hillside," the prince said, "please, before we take another fall."

Hodge gave his back for support, and though Prince Leo gasped with each jarring movement, they were able to hop-step the rest of the way down the hill. Finally, the prince was settled in the shade of an oak tree.

"Your leg?" Hodge asked. "How is it?"

The prince tried to ease himself to a more comfortable position. "I-I think I've made it worse."

Hodge shook his head. His anxiety for Fleet pulled at him. "I must get back to Castle Marlby. My brother."

The prince grimaced. "Certainly. But evening is coming on. Perhaps you could start a fire before you leave." He shivered. "I've taken a bit of a chill."

Hodge cast a look down the valley. The trees and bushes turned indistinct in the twilight. "All right, but then I'm going."

Soon a yellow blaze pushed back the shadows. A hint of autumn air brushed across Hodge's face. The fire's warmth felt good, with the sun gone beyond the hills.

"It's getting dark," Prince Leo said. "There is still some bread in the bag. You should eat before you go."

Hodge's growling stomach reminded him that his last meal had been early that morning. "Maybe a little."

He divided the remaining loaf between them. Though their meal consisted of nothing more than stale bread and water, Hodge tore into his share with gusto.

The prince washed his food down with sips from his flask. "How old do you suppose this world is?" he asked after a bit, catching Hodge with a mouth full.

It was a strange question. Hodge swallowed and then broke off another piece of bread. He thought back over the stories Jesper had told—stories of long-dead kings and musty old knights. "A hundred years?" To him that seemed forever.

Prince Leo laughed. He took another drink. "My grand-father had a horse that lived that long. Sir Greyling they called him." He laughed again. "No, this world is older than that. Ancient beyond memory." He paused to belch. "Ancient beyond stories." He rested his head back against the tree trunk and closed his eyes. "Ancient beyond . . . beyond thought."

Hodge stirred the fire with a stick. "Fleet told me once—" But then he fell silent, his memory of that distant time troubled by the recollection of Fleet's current danger.

"What did Fleet tell you?"

"Nothing."

"What pearls of wisdom did your brother have to offer?"

Hodge wished the prince would leave him be.

"What great mysteries did he share with you?"

Hodge slapped the stick into the coals, sending up a shower of sparks into the darkness overhead. "He said you were not to be trusted!"

"Ahhh, then your brother is wise beyond his years. There is not much worthy of trust in this old world. Why, I expect it's older even than truth."

The prince leaned forward over his injured leg. "Ah, it hurts when I think." He took another drink from the flask. "How I wish this water were wine."

Hodge stared into the blaze. After a bit he stood to stretch his legs. Evening had given way to night. Prince Leo had curled up between two great oak roots and had already fallen asleep, as if the water had indeed been wine. His snores were audible over the crackling of the fire.

Though Hodge yearned for the castle and his brother, he remained to watch over Prince Leo—only till morning, he promised himself. Only till first light. Then he would be off.

He found a spot near the fire, amongst the ferns, and curled up himself.

✦ ✦ ✦

That night Hodge dreamed of Bilda—a pleasant dream of food and warmth and bustling noise. Bilda, the center of it all, directed the kitchen staff as if it were an army. The ovens steamed with a hundred loaves of baking bread, a thousand roasting fowl turned on spits over roaring fires, and a cheerful light flickered through it all, painting their faces golden with its glow. Bilda shouted a warning. With a boom, the ovens cracked open. Their fiery contents spilled across the floor: crumpled forms and tangled banners—men in battered armor that shone red in the blaze.

Hodge staggered back as the ovens disgorged themselves, filling the kitchen with the corpses of those he knew: Sir Granby, Lord Selden, Fleet. . . .

"No!" Hodge cried as he jerked awake.

"What is it?" said a voice.

Bewildered, Hodge looked around, trying to recollect himself. Daylight slanted through the trees. Bird calls echoed down the valley, mingling with the gentle chatter of the brook.

"Are you all right?" Prince Leo asked. He sat slumped beneath the oak.

"It was only a dream," Hodge said, shaking his head. "Just a dream." He shuddered at the memory.

"Ah. My dreams trouble me as well."

But it wasn't the dream that bothered Hodge now. "I must go. My brother—"

The prince leaned forward, fixing his blurry eyes on Hodge. "Take me with you."

"No. There isn't time." Hodge clambered to his feet. "The castle may already have fallen."

"Yes, it may have. Lord Pertwie is cunning. Don't let him capture you again. He will be disappointed that you did not allow his man to complete his task."

"I'll be careful." Hodge took a drink from the stream and splashed water on his face to wash away the last remnants of nightmare.

"Good luck," the prince said.

CHAPTER SIXTEEN

*H*odge had seen death before, laid out in the castle chapel with lilies and crushed roses, attended by chants and prayers and wisps of incense. He had seen death in the village, wreathed with mint leaves and daisies and accompanied by tears. He had seen death take those at both ends of life and everywhere in between.

Yet though he had seen death and knew its face, what scattered the field today horrified him. This was not simply dying, but a twisted, garish violence that left blood seeping into the earth and a sour smell in the air. What he saw had no place in his experience, no basis in reality, so he tried to shut it out, focusing instead on Castle Marlby in the distance. Even so, wings of darkness fluttered just at the edges of thought.

Something terrible had happened here. Now, except for the crows' pecking and squawking, silence lay upon a battlefield that had grown up overnight. No movement disrupted the ghastly calm upon the plain. The battle was over, the day was won.

But by whom? Hodge wondered. *By whom?*

The only clues amongst the corpses that littered the field were broken and trampled banners, some the silver and green of Lord Pertwie, others the yellow and red of the royal household—the king's own forces. But no victory banner of any kind flew from the castle tower. No shouts of triumph echoed across the plain. Hodge's heart turned over in his chest, and his knees weakened as he picked his way through the bodies of horses and men. He would have sunk to the ground but for the gore already strewn about.

With each step toward the castle his apprehension grew. In places, the gray stones of the outer wall had tumbled into the moat. The high tower leaned, tottering toward collapse. The gatehouse was in ruins.

Hodge wondered if he had somehow wandered back into his early morning dream. The fortress that had been his home, his world, had seemed everlastingly strong and alive. Now the hulking pile reminded him of a skull picked clean by crows. He staggered, nearly falling. The metallic taste in his mouth startled him. He had bitten his lip. He spat out the blood and hurried toward the castle gate.

"Fleet!" he cried as he scrambled over the drawbridge. It had broken loose from its chains and crashed into place, scattering splinters across the paving stones.

"Fleet!"

He climbed through the ruin of the gatehouse, heaving aside timbers and charred beams.

"Fleet!"

He raced across the court to the Great Hall.

"Brother, where are you?"

He hurried to the mews, but all he found was a smoking rubble. He poked through the debris, fearful of what might lie beneath. He thought he recognized the carcass of old Titus the tiercel. He untied the bird from its jesses and lifted the charred body out of the ashes. With the falcon clutched to his chest, he moved on to the kitchen.

"Brother?" he called through the open door.

"He's gone," said a voice. "Fleet's gone." It was Bilda.

Hodge entered the darkness, squinting to adjust his eyes. "Where is he?"

Bilda sat on a low stool, her skirts billowed out about her. A girl sat on the floor beside her, resting her head on Bilda's lap. It was Jayne Kemp.

Bilda stroked Jayne's auburn hair. "Your brother is gone," Bilda said, "with most everyone else. And m'Lord is dead. And Sir Granby and Sir William are gone. And the battle is over." She looked up. "And here you come asking for your brother like yesterday wasn't the devil's own."

"But where did he go? I've got to find him."

Bilda shrugged. Then she whispered to Jayne in words that Hodge could barely hear. "We must bake some bread, my dear. And then cook up a fine stew, though not so much as before. Just enough for the few of us."

Jayne raised her head and nodded. Her face was wet with crying. Hodge touched his own cheek and pulled away glistening fingers. He struggled to remember when his weeping had begun.

"What battle?" he asked. "What happened on the field? Was the king here?"

"Does it matter?"

"Besides, they've all gone." It was Bert the ostler who startled Hodge from behind. "Both damn armies, all gone." He trudged down the steps into the kitchen. A dark stain spread across the front of his jerkin. "But they've left their dead and dying."

"You're hurt," Hodge said.

Bert shook his head. "Nah. This ain't my blood."

Hodge held out the falcon he still clutched in one hand. "Have you seen Fleet?" he asked.

Bert shook his head. "Fleet's long gone. He went out lookin' for you yesterday, when the king's army came and drew that other scoundrel's attention away from us. 'Fraid you was killed, Fleet said. Guess you wasn't. All this for a damn prince who wasn't even here."

Bilda raised Jayne to her feet. "Here, Bert," she said to the ostler, "build us a fire." She glanced at Hodge. "And you, fetch me a coney from the hutches, if they haven't all burned up. And onions and turnips from the cellar. I'm getting hungry. And Jayne, my dear. Fetch us some water from the well."

Jayne opened her mouth to speak, but Bilda hushed her. "Don't fret. There'll be nothing falling from the sky this morning."

✦ ✦ ✦

The smells of baking bread and simmering stew almost made Hodge think his world hadn't been shattered to a million pieces. It was a pleasant conceit to close his eyes and breathe and pretend that this meal was for the entire castle household. The usual chaotic music of the kitchen, however, was gone. Bilda spoke to Jayne in quiet tones instead of barking commands. And Jayne hung close about when she wasn't off to fetch some required ingredient. Bilda didn't seem to mind.

Hodge helped by cutting up the coney meat. Bert fell asleep in the corner, head back against the wall. The blood on his shirt had dried to a dark brown. Hodge wanted to question him about the battle, but he hesitated to bother the cantankerous man.

At midday, Bilda heaved the simmering pot onto the table along with several loaves of fresh-baked bread. To Jayne she said, "A full stomach'll dry that face of yours."

Jayne nodded and drew her seat next to Bilda's.

While they ate, Hodge mustered up his courage. "Tell me more about Fleet. Where did he go?"

Bert wiped his mouth on his sleeve before he answered. "Your brother said he was gonna meet up with the king's army. Thought with them he'd have a better chance of finding you. I told him you was likely dead. By then m'Lord was killed—arrow through the throat while he was standing up on the wall. So there was only me to stop Fleet a-goin' off. I figured if he wanted to get himself killed, too, then that was his own concern. When he snuck out the broken gate, there was already armies all over the field. When the fightin' started, I figured he was a dead 'un, for sure."

"The king's men came to save the castle? Who won the battle? Where are they?"

"D'ya think if the king was victorious we'd be sittin' here all alone, eating to our heart's content, instead of running about trying to feed all them royal people?"

Hodge peeked over the table and shrugged his shoulders. "Perhaps not," he said.

"Aye, and that's a blessing," said Bilda.

✦ ✦ ✦

Not more than an hour later, Hodge climbed up on the outer wall to survey the surrounding fields. This side of the castle was spared much of the damage, and Hodge imagined that if he stood across the moat and looked back the castle would appear almost whole, just as when he had left.

He leaned his head against the cool stones and remembered climbing the high tower long ago, when he was a little child. It was a distant recollection of clambering up interminable stairs on short legs, circling round and round until he burst out into the sky itself. He had been running away from something—he couldn't remember what, only that he had been crying. Fleet had followed after him. Together they stood at the top of the tower and gazed at the wide world. Fleet pointed out the patchwork of distant hills and forests until Hodge forgot his tears. Remembering his brother now almost brought the tears back.

Hodge heaved himself up between the merlons. A fluff of white caught his attention—a feather, stuck to the rough stonework. He pulled the feather loose and let it flutter away into the open air. Picked up by the breeze that blew at his back, the feather spiraled across the moat and out onto the field where the battle had left behind many dead soldiers. The thought that Fleet could have been one of them made Hodge shudder.

He gazed down at the moat, trying to drive out the unwelcome image. He wondered what had happened to his wings. He thought if he had them still, he would jump again. But this time he wouldn't follow the prince. Instead, maybe he would just disappear with the wings into the thick, black waters.

Standing in the space between the merlons, feeling as if the whole world were pushing down on him, he raised his eyes to the north. According to Bert, the king's army had retreated that way, pursued by Lord Pertwie's soldiers. Hodge shook his head.

Fleet might as well be dead for all the chance Hodge had of seeing him again. Long ago, when he stood sobbing on the castle tower, Fleet had told him the world was a great wide place, a place to lose oneself. Now it was Fleet who was lost, and only Hodge was left to find him. Suddenly he remembered why he had run to the tower so long ago. Bilda had threatened to give him a bath.

He knelt to lower himself back to the wall walk. Shielding his face from the afternoon sun, he took a last look at the wooded hills. A figure moved there in the distance, hobbling onto the battlefield. Hodge squinted, trying to make out its form: a man, moving slowly, supported by a tree branch, hopping on one leg as he threaded his way through the fallen warriors.

Even without seeing the blue of his eyes, Hodge knew who it was.

CHAPTER SEVENTEEN

I'm going to find my brother," Hodge announced as he stepped into the kitchen. "He's gone somewhere, and I'm going to find him." Though it seemed an impossible task, Hodge had made up his mind.

"You'd be best off to search the field first," Bert said. "Save you a long journey."

"No!" Hodge had already made up his mind about that, too. "Fleet's not there. He can't be."

Bert shrugged. "Would save you a trip even so."

"But it would take time," said Jayne in a soft voice. It was the first Hodge had heard her speak since his return. She and Bilda had finished cleaning up and now sat near the open hearth. Though late summer still hung about, Bert had kindled a small blaze for them.

Jayne raised her eyes from the fire to look at Hodge. "And if Fleet is—" She took a deep, shuddering breath. "Well . . . if he is killed, there'll be time enough to find out later."

Hodge had also thought that through. He nodded. As long as he searched, there was hope.

Bert stood up. "Pah! You're both fools." He trudged up the steps out of the kitchen.

Jayne buried her face in Bilda's shoulder and shook with sobs.

"There, that's all right, dear," Bilda said, pulling her close. "Go ahead and have another cry."

She looked at Hodge. "Jayne's own dear Thomas was found dead, out on the field. They was to marry this very fall."

"Tom Dalby?"

Bilda nodded.

The thought of his old tormentor dead seemed more than Hodge could bear. He racked his mind for some words of comfort to speak to Jayne but nothing seemed adequate. "I'm sorry," he finally mumbled.

Bert returned to the kitchen after only a moment.

"Someone's comin' through the gate," he said.

"Who is it?" Bilda asked.

"Don't know, but they're a noisy lot."

Hodge had a good idea who it might be. "Prince Leo," he said.

Bert peered back out the door. "Who?"

"Prince Leo. I saw him coming across the field a bit ago."

"How could that be?"

"He's been up in the hills, hiding."

"Well, why didn't you say somethin'?" Bert spat on the kitchen steps. "So His Highness *is* here—the man who damned us all! Maybe I'll just get out there and pay my respects. Show him some . . ." Bert paused with his lip curled in a snarl, ". . . some honor."

"No," Hodge said. "There's no need. He's already hurt."

"Hurt? Look around you, boy! Where's your brother? Where's Lord Selden? Where's my Elspie? I tell you, it's that traitor what's done it!" Bert disappeared out the door.

Hodge hurried to follow. Afternoon had settled in, casting imperfect shadows from the damaged walls and towers. The smell of burning hung in the air. A grimy figure stumbled from the gatehouse, bent nearly double as he leaned upon his staff and lurched into the courtyard. Spying Hodge, the figure sank to the ground.

"At last!" the prince cried. "I despaired of finding you."

Hodge could only stare at him.

"Please, tell me the news," the prince called in a hoarse voice. "What has happened?"

Bert strode grumbling toward the stables. "All hell has happened," he growled. He cast a dark look at the prince, then disappeared through the stable entrance.

"That's the prince?" Jayne asked. She stood just behind Hodge, red-nosed and sniffling. She wiped her eyes with the back of her hand.

Hodge nodded.

"Is what Bert said true?" Jayne asked. "Is it his doing?"

Hodge shrugged.

"He doesn't look like a traitor," Jayne whispered.

"No, he doesn't." Hodge clenched his fists, angry at having given so much sympathy to this man. "Looks can deceive." He shook his head. "Well, come on, help me with him."

✦ ✦ ✦

Hodge and Jayne stood at the bottom of the long flight of stairs, supporting the exhausted prince between them.

"Where should we put him?" Jayne asked.

"He *is* the prince," Hodge said. "We should take him to the solar."

Prince Leo shifted his weight onto Jayne's shoulders. "Is there aught for supper?" he asked.

Jayne pushed a strand of hair from her face. "Hurry, then. I can scarcely hold him up."

The prince leaned back on Hodge's hunched frame. "And a change of clothes?"

"Come on," Hodge said. "Lift your foot up the first step."

"And a bath?"

"Now the next step," Jayne said.

After many halts and much encouragement, Hodge and Jayne at last deposited the prince on his bed.

While Jayne scurried off to fetch something to eat and drink, Hodge helped Prince Leo out of his torn and dirty clothes. It was difficult removing the boot from his injured leg, but he gritted his teeth and allowed Hodge to pull the boot until it slipped off his foot.

Hodge handed the prince a clean nightshirt from the wardrobe and helped him settle into bed.

Jayne returned with a bowl of warmed-over stew.

Prince Leo nearly buried his face in the bowl as he shoveled the food into his mouth. "Seems like forever since I've had anything properly cooked," he muttered between gulps.

Hodge offered the prince a cup of water. "I'll be leaving soon to find my brother," he said. "You'll be safe here while I'm gone."

The prince paused from his eating to take the cup. Gravy dribbled over his chin. Hodge thought back to the first time he had seen the prince. He had seemed so tall and handsome, with his flashing blue eyes and neatly trimmed beard. Now his beard was ragged and his hair disheveled. The dark circles beneath his eyes brought the only color to his pale, drawn face. Though his looks had changed, his manners had not. As Hodge watched, Prince Leo wiped his chin on the sleeve of his nightshirt and belched.

"Your brother isn't here?"

Hodge shook his head. "I have to find him."

"I wish you luck."

After gulping the water, Prince Leo once again buried his face in the bowl. When he finished, Jayne handed him a wet towel to clean his face and hands. He mumbled his thanks. Jayne curtsied and hurried back to the kitchen with the empty bowl.

✦ ✦ ✦

It was Bilda who set matters straight concerning the prince. "We'll not be tending him," she said. "If you want him safe, take him with you."

Hodge shook his head. "I can't. I'll never find Fleet with him hobbling along behind."

Bert growled from the kitchen corner. "If you leave him here, *I'll* take care of him, that's for damn sure. And there's more like me." He spat into the fire. "Now that the armies are gone, some of the village folk have come back. And Nat Cooper, what lost his son to the mangonels. They'll be more, too. Between us, we'll see to him."

The threat in Bert's voice sent an icy stab through Hodge's chest. "What'll you do?"

"I'd say there's a tower with his name graven on it. A high tower, too."

"Hanging?"

Bert laughed a harsh, unpleasant laugh. "Only for a bit."

"I'll not be having that talk in my kitchen," Bilda said. "You clear out, Bert, if you can't be civil."

Bert growled again and stomped up the steps into the evening shadows.

"He wouldn't do that!" Jayne said. "Would he?" She seemed as upset by Bert's words as Hodge.

Bilda shook her head. "I don't know. Once those men are gone in their ale, they might have the courage to do most anything. Not that I blame them over much."

Hodge slammed his fist into the sack of flour on which he sat, sending up a puff of dust. "I *can't* take him with me. I've got to find my brother."

"Then you best be off," Bilda said. " 'Stead of just sitting there talking about it."

✦ ✦ ✦

Hodge decided to set out first thing in the morning. He figured the trail of scores of men and horses should be easy enough to follow. He would leave at first light. Bilda prepared a sack of victuals that he could carry slung over his back. Jayne had rounded up a couple of water skins for him.

That night Hodge slept in the kitchen, curled up by the hearth in a blanket. The weather had turned cooler, and the dying embers felt good at his back. Anxious for the day, Hodge only dozed, measuring the night's passage by his own restlessness. At last he felt a deeper sleep settling into his brain.

"Hsst! Boy, wake up!"

Hodge sat up in alarm. "What? What is it?"

He recognized Bilda's face in the candle's flickering glow. She was dressed for bed, with a woolen shawl thrown haphazardly over her shoulders.

"I fear they're coming to take your prince," she said.

Hodge tried to shake the sleep from his head. "Who is?"

"It's those men. Bert and Nat and some others I don't recognize. I heard their noise. They've been drinking Lord Selden's brandy and talking big. That's always trouble. I fear they plan some harm."

Hodge jumped up. "Where are they?"

"They've gathered in the stables. You best get your prince away from here, unless you want to see him swinging from that tower."

Before Hodge knew what was happening, he found himself scurrying up the great stairs toward Prince Leo, wondering why he couldn't just turn his back and leave.

CHAPTER EIGHTEEN

*H*odge had trouble rousing the prince. After several unsuccessful shakes, he thought he might have to pinch the prince awake. Finally, however, Prince Leo groaned and raised his head in the darkness.

"What is it?" he asked. "Why won't you let me sleep?"

"There's danger. Bert thinks you're a traitor. He wants to hang you."

"He wouldn't dare."

"Bilda says he might. And there's others with him. They blame you for all that's happened."

"But—"

"There's no time. Please, get up. You've got to get away." Hodge tugged on the prince's arm, pulling him to a sitting position. "Here's your clothes."

He hurried to the door and peeked out. Nothing stirred in the dark hallway. Hodge returned to the bed. "Please, Your Highness! Get your clothes on."

With Hodge's frantic urging, Prince Leo gave up complaining and dressed himself in the garments that Hodge had rummaged from the wardrobe, even tugging a boot onto his injured leg.

"Now what?" he asked, still panting from the effort.

"Shhh," Hodge hissed. "I heard something."

A rustling sound came from near the doorway.

"Who's there?" Hodge asked.

"It's only me," answered a soft voice. Jayne appeared out of the darkness. "I've come to help."

Together Hodge and the prince breathed a sigh of relief.

"I thought it was Bert," said Hodge. "I thought we were discovered."

"Not yet, but soon." Jayne crept back into the hall. "It's all clear," she whispered.

In a few moments the three stood at the top of the stairs.

"Going down will be easier," Jayne said. She pulled the prince's arm over her shoulder. "Just one step at a time."

Hodge noticed she was fully dressed and covered in a traveling cloak. "Are you going somewhere?" he asked.

Jayne ignored his question. "Just one step at a time," she repeated.

Hodge allowed Prince Leo to lean on his back and together the three descended toward the Great Hall. Bilda waited at the foot of the long flight, a candle clutched in one hand and a large ring of iron keys in the other.

"To the postern," she said. "Through the kitchen. If we hurry, they'll not see us."

She led the way across the Hall and through the buttery, shining the candle before them. "Get your things," she said to Hodge.

He gathered up his pack from the kitchen corner where he had left it. Bilda snuffed out the candle. In her nightclothes she looked like a billowing ghost as she floated to the outer door. She paused to peer into the moonlit night.

"Come now."

She led the way along the wall.

Hodge glanced toward the stable. Firelight flickered from beneath its thatched roof. Rough voices echoed across the courtyard, then shouts and angry oaths.

"Hurry," Bilda said. "I do believe they've decided."

Nearly dragging the prince, they ducked out of sight around the corner of the keep, then skirted the well and passed through the gateway into the outer ward.

Bilda took them straight to the postern. She held the ring of keys up in the moonlight and selected the largest one. Kicking through the weeds that choked the doorway, she pushed the key into the rusty lock.

"You had those all along," Hodge said. "I should have known."

"Lord Selden had them," Bilda answered. "But I thought with him dead . . ."

The lock clicked. Bilda knocked it open with the flat of her hand.

"Now what?" Prince Leo asked. "I'm certainly not up to slogging over the fields."

The heavy door squealed as Bilda pushed her weight against it. "Just wait out here for a bit."

She disappeared back into the inner courtyard of the castle.

"We'd best do as she says," Jayne said, moving through the gateway.

Hodge looked at the full moon rising above the keep. "It must be after midnight." He stepped through the postern, helping Prince Leo after him.

"Only just," Jayne said.

She pushed at the door, trying to close it behind them. It wouldn't budge. Hodge set his own shoulder against its oak planks. It squeaked as it moved an inch or two, then stopped. He nervously peered along the pathway that skirted the moat and the castle wall. Like the sally port, it too was overgrown with weeds and rank grass.

"So we just wait here?" Prince Leo asked.

"That's what Bilda said," Jayne answered.

"*You* don't need to wait," Hodge said. "You could go back inside where it's safe."

Jayne shook her head. "I'm going with you."

"What? You can't go with me."

"I can."

"Bilda would never—"

"She agrees I should."

"But it's dangerous out there." Hodge cast his arm about in the darkness. "It's a wild place."

Jayne snorted, her soft voice turning hard. "Nor is it better here. Not for a maiden, with m'Lord gone and only rough men about."

Prince Leo sank to the ground. "She's right," he said, rubbing his injured leg. "Some men are not to be trusted."

"Besides," she said, "you'll need my help."

"I don't like it." Hodge slumped against the stone wall. "How am I ever going to find my brother?"

✦ ✦ ✦

Bilda returned moments later with a donkey in tow. "This will have to do," she said as she pushed the door wider. "While those toad-heads were busy rummaging about inside, I managed to sneak him from the stable." She laughed and shook her head. "The drink that swells their courage also causes great blindness."

"Do you mean for me to ride that?" Prince Leo asked.

"The horses are gone," Bilda said. "It's either the ass or your feet. Now hurry." She threw her arms about Jayne and lifted her off the ground in an embrace. "May God go with you," she said. Then she thumped Hodge on the shoulder. "Take care of my girl. And boy—" She ruffled his hair. "Take care of yourself. I hope you find your Fleet."

After helping the prince onto the donkey, Bilda pulled in her stomach and sidled through the gateway. She leaned back with all her weight and pulled the heavy oak door closed. The scrape of the bolt being shoved into place and the clanking snap of the lock sent a shiver through Hodge's insides that stayed with him throughout the remainder of that long and fearful night.

PART III

The Wide World

Love, tarry yet a while.

CHAPTER NINETEEN

*J*esper once told a story of a great battle that took place before the beginning of time, when men fought with nothing more than stone axes and bare hands. Clad in animal skins and fur boots, the savage armies raged across the entire world, leaving their dead and wounded to litter the ground. The battle ended only when the last two warriors had been slain.

In a low and hollow voice, Jesper told how their million ghosts were cursed to haunt the earth's battlefields for all eternity, following behind the crows to pick through the bones of the dead and collect their souls.

As Hodge led the way across the darkened plain, he wished he could put that story out of his mind. But try as he might, every whisper of a windblown banner, every rustle through the trampled grass reminded him that new ghosts had swollen the number of the cursed.

He took a deep breath. Thin clouds scudded against the full moon, turning silver in its light. A pale glow seemed to rise up from the field about them.

"Be careful," Hodge called back to Jayne. "Stay close to the donkey. He knows where to step."

"Hodge, I'm afraid."

"They're only dead men," Prince Leo said. "They can't hurt you."

Hodge understood Jayne's fear. It wasn't the thought of pain that filled him with panic. It was the thought that in the midst of all this death they were not alone, that empty eyes watched their passage with envy.

"It's all right," he said, as much for his benefit as for Jayne's. "We'll be through soon enough."

But his words seemed a lie. It was as if they had gone back in time to the battlefield of Jesper's story—the battlefield that had covered the whole earth. Though they moved onward, the scene about them remained unchanged: dark corpses scattered the ground, bits of weapons and armor glinted in the moonlight, and a chilling breeze snaked through it all like a ghost itself. Hodge felt as if he was wandering in a dream.

"Hodge!" Jayne called. "Watch out!"

He stumbled and fell to the ground. It seemed that

something must have reached out to trip him. He jumped to his feet. "I'm all right."

"Be careful," Prince Leo said. "I'll not have you breaking a leg, too. There isn't room up here for the both of us."

Hodge shivered and wiped his hands on his jerkin. He allowed Jayne to catch up to him. "The sun will be rising soon," he whispered.

Jayne nodded.

"And then we can stop for breakfast," the prince said.

But the sun didn't come up soon. The night only darkened as clouds gathered to envelop the moon, making it impossible to gauge the passage of time. Hodge led the donkey and Jayne followed closely behind. The ground gradually rose before them, and at long last they left the churned earth of the plain with its smell of death. A breeze kicked up, blowing cold as it shifted out of the north.

"A storm is coming," Hodge said.

Jayne pulled her cloak close about her. "We'll need to find shelter."

"At first light we can find a place to rest."

"I believe His Highness is already resting."

Prince Leo slumped forward on the donkey, his chin on his chest.

Hodge shook his head. "What am I going to do with him? I can't take him about the whole world while I look for Fleet."

The prince jerked awake. "What? Where are we?"

✦ ✦ ✦

No welcome sunrise brought a blush of dawn to the gray sky that morning. No warming rays burned away the chill of night. Instead, a watery light seeped into the air to reveal an unfamiliar landscape. For the last hour or so, Hodge had been stumbling along in a sleepy fog, nearly unconscious with fatigue. He had paid little heed to the growing light, until a shiver made him wish for the sun itself.

"It's going to rain," he said.

He glanced back at Jayne and the prince. "We must find someplace where we can keep dry."

"No caves," Prince Leo said. "I'm done with caves."

Hodge scanned the countryside. A wide valley spread before him, hemmed in on either side by rolling hills. A fold of land jutted into the valley ahead, covered by a stand of twisted trees.

"Maybe there, upon that ridge."

"Yes," Jayne said. "The trees might give us shelter."

"And wood for a fire," the prince added. "And a place for breakfast."

"And a good hiding place," Hodge said.

He led the way, trudging through the late summer grass. Perhaps sensing an end to its long, burdened night, the donkey bolted ahead.

"Whoa," Hodge cried. He nearly fell to his face as the halter jerked from his hands.

Jayne laughed—a musical laugh that echoed in the damp air. "Be careful. You don't want the donkey choosing our camp."

"No, nor me neither," cried the prince, clutching the animal's neck.

The donkey, realizing its freedom, slowed, then stopped altogether. It lowered its head to the grass and tore up a mouthful.

Hodge looked into the gray clouds and blinked. A misting rain had begun. "I'll find a place."

After a quick search he located a sheltered spot near the crest of the ridge, beneath a pair of tangled trees. Years of fallen leaves formed a soft bed, and a roof of leaves overhead offered protection from the wet. Even the donkey found room beneath the branches.

"You chose well," Prince Leo said. "Though I would still prefer a fire."

"I don't think it's safe to have a fire. Who knows where Lord Pertwie is."

"I've blankets," Jayne said, producing a bag she carried beneath her cloak. She pulled out a pair of woolen blankets and handed one to the prince. "And some biscuits."

Hodge sank down to the ground and tugged his own blanket from his pack. "We should rest. I'm so tired I could sleep a fortnight."

"No," Prince Leo said. "We should eat."

Hodge nodded. "Yes. Eat, then sleep. And then move on. There's two days to make up if I'm to find my brother."

◆ ◆ ◆

By the time Hodge awoke the rain had stopped, though lowering clouds still hid the sky. He let Jayne and the prince sleep on while he crept to the crest of the ridge, then followed it down to emerge from the trees. He clambered atop a damp outcropping of rock and scanned the valley, looking back the way they had come and searching the path that lay ahead. Now that his mind was refreshed he realized something was wrong. Something was missing—something even the rain shouldn't have been able to wash away.

He raced back to their camp.

"The armies of the king," he said, "there's no sign of their passage. We must have gone astray in the dark!"

CHAPTER TWENTY

*W*hy do you want to follow my father's army?"
Prince Leo asked.

"To find my brother," Hodge said. "Bert told me he is
with them."

The prince shook his head. "You're more apt to find Pertwie along that path. If you want to meet up with the king
you'll have to find out where the royal muster is to be held.
That is where all his armies will gather after the defeat
they've suffered. They will regroup and swell their numbers.
Seems Pertwie had his chance, but he let the king escape."

Hodge slumped against the tree trunk and dug his
hands into the moldering leaves. "The royal muster? Where's
that? How would I ever find it?" He felt dizzy at the sudden immensity of the world.

Prince Leo fell silent. He pulled his blanket closer about his shoulders.

Hodge looked at Jayne. "Where do we go now? How can I find Fleet?"

"I don't know," Jayne said. "I wish Bilda were here."

At last the prince cleared his throat. "Caerlendon," he said. "You'll find them there." He ran his fingers through his unkempt hair. "It appears all my choices are evil. I can either face my father or deal with Lord Pertwie."

"What do you mean?" Hodge asked.

"I'll take you to him."

"You'd take us to your father's army?"

Prince Leo gave Hodge an indignant look. "You've saved me thrice. I'm not a complete scoundrel."

"I'm sorry. I didn't mean—"

The prince waved him silent. "Yes, you did. I know what you think of me. I'm a coward and a traitor. I plotted against my father. Men have died because of me. You hate me, but yet—" He sighed. "But yet you're stuck with me."

Hodge had no words for that.

Jayne interrupted the awkward silence. "How far is it to this place?"

"Caerlendon? I'm not sure. Our journey last night put us several leagues out of the way, but if we head east we'll strike the Bandit's Highway soon enough. Don't let its name fool you. It's not much more than a cow path, barely wide enough for a wagon. Then we go north. It's wild country between here and there. Not so pleasant as this."

Hodge shivered in the damp air. Though the green canopy had kept them out of the rain, drops of water still trickled through the leaves to splatter about them.

"Well, we best be on our way."

✦ ✦ ✦

Hodge had never heard Jayne sing by herself before. Though he remembered her joining in the boisterous caroling around the winter fires of the Great Hall, her voice had always blended with the others. Now, as they trudged over the forested hills, she began to hum, as if to try and cheer herself. Though plain and unadorned, her voice made Hodge think of all the things he had left behind: the summer fields of grain, the splashing brook, the high towers and protecting walls.

"What's that song?" he asked.

Jayne seemed to come to herself from far away. "Oh, it's nothing."

"It's lovely," said the prince from atop the donkey. "Do go on."

"It's only a little tune," she said. "I'm not much of a singer."

"Please," Hodge said. "I would like to hear more."

"Yes, do," said the prince. "I don't believe I know that melody."

Jayne's lip trembled. "It . . . it's the song that won my Tom."

"Oh." Hodge felt ashamed for pressing her so. "I'm sorry."

"Who's Tom?" the prince asked.

"Tom is dead," Hodge whispered. "They were to wed this fall."

"Oh. I, too, am sorry."

When Jayne sang again, her voice was thin and airy, as if it might flutter away on the breeze.

O, bonnie lad
Why goest thou sad
With countenance forlorn?
Canst hear yon birds
Their warbling words
To secrets ne'er forsworn?
O, gentle youth
'Tis of a truth
A grief to be alone.
I'd not refuse
E'en thou woulds't choose
To have me for thine own.

Her song faltered, and she fell silent.

"We're off track," Prince Leo said, glancing back at the

sun, which had at last broken through the clouds. "We're heading too much to the north."

Hodge corrected his path so that the dappled shadows stretched straight before them.

As they forged ahead, the land flattened, though movement became more difficult. Thick underbrush clogged the spaces between the crowding oak and sycamore trees. Heavy branches began to block out the afternoon. Hodge now had to take a winding trail through the gloomy forest. That evening found them huddled within the hollow trunk of a tumbled giant.

"Are there wolves in these woods?" Jayne asked.

"I've never known a wolf to harm a man," Prince Leo said. "Or woman. However, this is wild country. There could be worse than wolves about. But come, we must rest. We have far to go tomorrow."

The prince wrapped his blanket about himself and was soon asleep. Hodge, however, could not seem to get comfortable. Every rustling of a leaf, every snap of a twig set him on edge. Jayne seemed to be restless, too.

"Are you asleep?" he asked after hearing her turn for what seemed the hundredth time.

"I'm not as tired as I thought," she said.

"Me neither. I miss my owl."

"Your owl?"

"Well, Fleet's and mine. He lived in our tower. Every night, just as we went to bed, he'd fly off on his hunt. He always lived backward from us, sleeping when we worked, working when we slept. I always said, 'Good hunting,' and he always obeyed me. I miss saying that."

"I miss my Tom," Jayne said.

Hodge could hear the tears in her voice, though he couldn't imagine how she had come to feel that way about Tom Dalby. "Was he kind to you?" he asked.

"Yes. . . ." She buried her sobbing into her blanket.

"I guess he was a fine enough man," Hodge said, trying to cheer her up. "He'd have to be. Not everyone would be worthy of your company. Not someone like me. Maybe Ren Cooper from the village, though perhaps he's too young—not yet twelve. Nat, his brother, is too old; besides, he's already married. But what if his wife died? No, you wouldn't want to marry a sad man. Maybe one of the Tolman twins, when they get older? Or a soldier? Maybe a knight. A girl like you could have your pick of anyone. Anyone at all. Even my brother, Fleet."

Hodge felt a hand touch his arm in the darkness.

"Thank you," Jayne whispered.

Hodge squirmed at the touch. "I wonder where my owl is now."

✦ ✦ ✦

"How much farther is this Robber's Road?" Hodge asked early the next morning. "I only packed food enough for me. There wasn't time to fetch more, except for the biscuits Jayne brought. I don't think we have enough."

"Bandit's Highway," Prince Leo corrected. "And don't worry, we'll find more food. There's bound to be a village or two along the way."

Hodge rummaged through the contents of his bag. "Not near enough," he mumbled.

"Why is it called the Bandit's Highway?" Jayne asked.

The prince laughed. "It's an ancient name. An ancient track. Don't worry, there are no *real* bandits anymore."

"And if there were," Hodge said, holding up a dry loaf of bread, "what could they want from us?"

The prince laughed again. "Yes, even our lives aren't worth much."

✦ ✦ ✦

Toward midmorning they crossed a boggy meadow. Though Hodge enjoyed the feel of open sunlight, annoying clouds of tiny flies swarmed about them, moving in gusts across their path. Hodge clamped his mouth shut and tried not to suck any of the pestering creatures up his nose.

Jayne swatted at the air, then stopped and pointed. "Look there." She spat out the insects that had darted into her mouth.

A thin column of smoke rose from the trees beyond the meadow.

Hodge hurried forward out of the swarm, pulling the donkey after him. "Is that a camp?"

"A village, just as I told you," the prince said. "That should solve our provender problem."

"Suppose they won't share?" asked Jayne.

"They will. After all, I am the prince."

Hodge shrugged. "Maybe they won't hold that against you."

The village was barely visible against the backdrop of trees. Thatched huts and primitive sheds blended in with the forest as if they had grown there along with the underbrush. The inhabitants in their coarse grays and browns also seemed a fixed part of the surroundings. They stood in a stupor and watched while Hodge, Jayne, and the prince entered the smoky clearing.

"Hello," Hodge called to a man who looked like a great, shaggy bear.

The man blinked and let his iron-headed ax drop to his side. From somewhere across the clearing, Hodge could hear the bleating of a goat. A thin woman emerged from a hut but stopped short upon spying Hodge and the donkey. A naked boy-child wormed his way past her. She grabbed him up and wiped his dirty face with her hand.

"What's that smell?" the prince asked, wrinkling up his nose.

"Swine," whispered Jayne.

As if in answer to her words, a large sow, snorting and snuffling, pushed its way out of the hut past the woman and child.

The bear-man took a step forward. Hodge raised his hand in greeting, but his words were interrupted by a whistling through the air. Something struck his thigh. He looked down. Still quivering, a rough-hewn arrow protruded from the thick muscle above his knee. A sudden pain flooded his body, and he collapsed to the ground.

"Hodge!" Jayne cried.

He tried to answer her, but though his mouth worked at the sound, nothing came out.

She floated into his vision. "What's happened?" And then she looked at his leg. "Hodge!"

"I got 'im," squeaked a voice from somewhere in the fuzzy distance.

Hodge reached for the arrow, but a large hand brushed his away.

"Let it be," growled a man.

Hodge looked up into a hairy face.

"Is he kill't?" asked the squeaking voice.

"Ye dolt!" the man called over his shoulder. "These ain't soldiers." He prodded the arrow wound. Hodge cried out in pain.

"Be careful!" said the prince. He slid off the donkey's back and hobbled to Hodge's side.

"Don't be afeard," said the bearded man. "It ain't broke the bone. It be only a stone tip. Though it go in a might messy, it'll come out clean enough."

And before Hodge could blink, the man clasped the arrow in both hands and jerked it from his leg.

CHAPTER TWENTY-ONE

*H*odge closed his eyes, trying to fight the imps that somersaulted through his stomach. He felt himself carried a short distance and set down. He sensed people hovering about. Though a rushing like a river continued to pulse in his ears, he opened his eyes. He could just make out the dim insides of a hut.

"Jayne?"

"I be Cull," said the hairy-faced man who knelt at his side.

"Where's Jayne?"

"I'm here."

"And I," said the prince.

"That wound needs to be wrapped," Cull said. "It's bleedin' a might bit."

"I'll tend to it," said Jayne. "But we'll need to get his breeches off."

"No!" Hodge cried, embarrassed at her attention. "I'll be all right."

Cull held him down. "Here now. Ye'll be wantin' to keep your blood on the inside, what ye can of it."

Within moments, Cull had pulled off Hodge's breeches. Jayne dressed the wound with moss and strips of cloth that Cull provided, while Prince Leo anxiously advised them on the dangers of a hurt left unattended.

"Aye," added Cull. "Ye don't want it to go a festerin' on ye. I've seen 'em turn black with putrefying afore. That dark curse can take a small hurt and wrap it up with death. Rest is what ye'll be needin'."

Hodge groaned. "But there's no time. I've got to find my brother."

A commotion from the doorway interrupted him before he had a chance to argue further. A boy stumbled into the hut, pushed from behind by the woman they had seen earlier. "Get on, Wat. Tell 'im."

The boy tugged at a lock of hair. He bobbed his head in a nervous half-bow. Even in the dim light, Hodge could see tears glistening in his eyes.

"I . . . I be *so* sorry." The boy cast a quick glance at Cull. "But . . . but I thought ye was them thievin' soldiers."

The woman prodded him in the back. "That be no excuse."

Wat hung his head. "No, there be no excuse. I waren't bein' chary. I shoulda held my arrow 'til I were sure."

"What soldiers?" Prince Leo asked.

Cull shook his head. "Men-at-arms what been through these woods, takin' what they want. Goin' someplace in a hurry. Not askin' leave nor beggin' pardon for what they take."

"Thievin' rascals," Wat said. "And I'm gonna put my arrow in one of 'em."

"Hsst, you rascal yourself," said the woman. "You leave off talkin' like that. You've already put your arrow in the wrong place. Now come on outta here. Leave these folk in peace."

Wat rushed forward and knelt at Hodge's side. "I be so sorry. Please, canst ye forgive me?"

Hodge nodded, embarrassed at the boy's begging. He thought he could understand the mistake. He'd had enough of soldiers himself. "I . . . I'll be all right."

Relief brightened Wat's face. He jumped up and backed out of the hut, bobbing and bowing with each step.

"Thank'ee," he said. Then he was gone.

Hodge looked at Jayne. "We've got to move on if I'm going to find my brother."

"But Hodge—"

"Yes," Prince Leo said. "We must hurry. With soldiers about in the woods, they must already be gathering for battle. We must get to Caerlendon before we miss them."

Cull grunted. "At least stay the night. Let the boy rest. Give the wound a chance to close." He looked at Prince Leo with an air of appraisal. He glanced at the prince's leg. "Besides, I'm thinkin' ye can't neither of you walk to anywhere soon. And ye've only one donkey."

"We could use the rest," Jayne said. "And the food."

Cull stood to leave. "You shall have both. And welcome to 'em."

He ducked from the hut and returned a short while later with a hearty stew full of strange roots and vegetables dished up in wooden bowls. Drink was poured from hollowed gourds. Hodge took a sip of the brownish liquid. It tasked like a bitter tree bark. The prince drained several cups of it before turning his attention to the stew.

"How be the leg doin'?" Cull asked.

"Better," Hodge said. He didn't dare tell them that it felt like a fire spreading up his thigh. "We should be able to leave in the morning."

✦ ✦ ✦

That night Hodge, Jayne, and the prince slept in the small hut. As Hodge lay in the darkness, he could just make out a glimmer of moonlight through the rough-thatched roof. Jayne's soft breathing made him think of Fleet and the last time they had talked together. His heart ached at the memory. He had told Fleet not to call him brother anymore. Now, after all that had happened, he wished he could unsay those words. He wished he could call back his fist. He wished he could return to the days before the arrival of the prince. But all those things were beyond his reach.

A tear rolled down his cheek. "Please, be alive," he whispered. "Please."

"Are you all right?" Prince Leo asked.

Hodge cleared his throat. He hadn't meant to speak aloud. "Y—yes. I'm fine."

"Good. You should try to get some sleep."

Hodge nodded in the darkness. "How are we going to get to Caerlendon? The donkey can't carry us both."

"Don't worry about that now. I've been thinking. Perhaps we should not be in such a hurry to get there after all."

"But . . . but why? You said—"

"Never mind what I said. Perhaps I've changed my mind. Now get some sleep. You need the rest."

After a while, Hodge broke the silence again. "Your Highness?"

"What?"

"Do you have a brother?"

Prince Leo didn't answer for the longest time. Hodge began to think he hadn't heard.

"Yes. I did." They were quiet words, spoken beneath the whispering darkness within the hut—spoken in a voice

Hodge had never heard before. "But he's dead. Now go to sleep."

✦ ✦ ✦

Hodge awoke in the early morning hours to a throbbing pain in his leg. With great difficulty he managed to push himself to his feet, but then he gave an anguished cry and collapsed back into his blankets.

Jayne hurried to his side. "Hodge, are you all right?"

"I can't walk. How will I find my brother if I can't walk?"

"Shhhhh." Her voice was soothing. "Your leg just needs a chance to heal."

Prince Leo limped across the dirt floor. "She's right," he said. "You must get well. I'll not have you dying. We will stay here until you can travel. Perhaps then *I* will be able to walk, and you can ride the donkey."

"No! My brother can't wait!" But he knew they were right. This forced delay made his mind rage, but his body felt weak and helpless. There was nothing he could do but wait.

Jayne stayed by his side through the day, helping ease the passing time. Cull brought in food. Though Hodge had no appetite for it, he ate what he could at the prince's urging.

The following day, his leg felt hot and the hurt had seemed to spread throughout his body, but he said nothing to the others about it. By the day after that, aching chills shivered through him.

Jayne was the first to notice his shaking and chattering. "Hodge, what's wrong?"

He tried to talk, but his words came out in muddled nonsense. He knew what he wanted to say, but his tongue refused to cooperate.

"His hurt has turned to fever," Cull said. He pulled a knife from his belt. "We'll be needin' to let the poison out." He handed the knife to Jayne. "I'll hold him down." He nodded to the prince. "Get Wat. Tell 'im I need the honey pot."

"Honey pot?"

"Aye! To salve the wound and fight the fever demons."

Jayne turned pale, staring at the knife in her hands. "I— I can't."

"You must. I'll guide ye."

Hodge struggled against Cull's grip. He heard a ripping sound as the bandages were cut from his wound. And then he felt a piercing blaze stab through his body.

Perhaps he screamed—or perhaps it was the cry of a falcon in the castle mews, impatient for its supper. Or perhaps he still lay in his own tower basement, curled up in blankets beside Fleet, sweating through this nightmare, impatient to awake to a bright summer's day. Perhaps it was all a dream.

CHAPTER TWENTY-TWO

A small corner of Hodge's mind wondered how long he would hover just on the edge of consciousness while the world turned about him. He knew time had passed, but much of what had happened was a blur. He remembered standing upon a high wall with wind blowing through a clumsy pair of wings. But that seemed forever ago. And longer still since he had rested within the safety of stone towers.

His eyelids felt glued shut. His hearing came from the depth of a well. He struggled awake, and was surprised to see golden daylight streaming through trees. He groaned.

A damp cloth was laid upon his forehead. "Shhhh," whispered a soft voice. "Rest easy."

"Jayne?"

"Yes, I'm here. You must lie still."

He closed his eyes. Yes, he would lie still. Movement was beyond him. Though the throbbing in his leg had subsided to a dull ache, he did not have the strength to stir. As he concentrated on the rise and fall of his chest, he heard other voices.

"How much farther to the Bandit's Highway?"

"We should be there afore evening. But we must move now."

A whisper of breath touched Hodge's ear. "I know this pains you," the soft voice said, "but soon you'll be able to rest comfortably. The prince says there's a surgeon at Caerlendon."

Hodge felt himself lifted in two large arms. "Wait, what about Fleet? I must find Fleet!"

The two arms held him fast against his struggling. Jayne reached up and touched him on the cheek. "Don't worry. Fleet will be waiting for you."

Hodge nodded weakly. Jayne's touch was reassuring. Fleet *would* be there.

Hodge became aware of the others. It was Cull who had lifted him as easily as if he were a sack of grain.

"Let's go," the big man said. He strode forward through the forest. Prince Leo bounced on the trotting donkey, led by the boy, Wat. Jayne stayed close to Cull and Hodge, almost running to keep up.

While they traveled, a fevered exhaustion pulled Hodge in and out of sleep. He was only dimly aware of their passage through trees, down a hill, across a stream. Late in the day he awoke to a wagon track that meandered toward the north. A film of dust coated the plants on either side of the road.

"This old path's seen a bit of traffic of late," said Cull. "We must be chary. Keep your eyes open."

"How much farther is it to Caerlendon?" asked the prince.

"Now, that I couldn't tell ye. They say there be a great wide world out there beyond this road, but I never cared to see it."

He laid Hodge down and glanced at the sky. "We can rest here 'til nightfall."

He sent Wat up the road a bit to spy out the way. Jayne helped Hodge drink from a water skin. He gulped the water down as if he would never get his fill.

"Be careful," Jayne warned. "It might make you ill."

He tried to eat, but the food caused his stomach to churn. After gagging on a small taste of bread, he gave up and contented himself with shivering under the blanket Jayne had wrapped about him.

At moonrise, Cull urged them up and on the trail again. "With a road to follow and a bit of moonlight we can go yet a ways, and perhaps get to this place of yours."

Though Hodge had slept through most of the day, he

still could not keep awake, especially now that they moved over an easy track instead of across rough forest terrain. Except for the occasional chill that rattled through him, he was oblivious to the passing night.

When he next awoke, it was to voices and burning torches. He struggled to free himself, recalling what seemed a long-ago nightmare of fire and destruction.

"Easy there, boy. We mean you no harm."

People gathered round—men in helmets and coats of chain mail. Faces moved in and out of his vision.

"Jayne," he called.

"I'm here." She clutched his hand.

"I've still got ye," Cull said.

"This way, to the surgeon's tent."

Hodge craned his neck to see where they were headed. A brazier burned brightly before a small pavilion, casting a flickering light upon the banners that stood on either side—billowing banners of silver and green.

✦ ✦ ✦

"So this is your pet," said a hauntingly familiar voice.

Hodge lay still on his cot, not daring to move. He had no desire to face Lord Pertwie again.

"See how he sleeps on," Lord Pertwie said. "A worthless bit of peasantry."

"I owe him my life—thanks to you."

"Oh, that. Well, it was worth a try, you understand."

"I understand, but now that's over and done. We have business to attend to."

"Yes. New business since you've been gone. As you are aware, your father has invited us to battle on the fields at Kingsfort. There, we will decide your ascendancy to the throne."

"You know we could never defeat all his gathered forces."

"Do you always do what your father wants? No, the way to topple a king is to strike at his heart."

"What do you mean?"

"While he is at Kingsfort, we simply attack his capital city. Once Warnick falls, the kingdom will be ours."

Hodge heard a humorless chuckle from the prince. "You *are* a rogue. But isn't it rather discourteous to bypass the king's army in the field and attack the people directly?"

"Why, yes. I do believe it is."

Hodge felt as if his heart had stopped, though blood still pounded in his ears. He clenched his fists and inadvertently groaned aloud.

"I believe your pet is coming around. You can thank my surgeon for saving him."

"It was Cull and the girl who saved him."

"What, that oaf?"

"Yes, *that* oaf. Where are they now?"

"They're being held under guard. When the girl realized this was not your father's camp, she became somewhat agitated. Don't worry, they are safe."

"But what about Hodge?"

"Is that his name? He must be a clever fellow to have wormed his way into your affection. But don't worry, my surgeon has said he will live. Now, come. We have plans to attend to."

"First, you have something that belongs to me."

"What? Oh, that. Yes, I suppose you'll be wanting it back."

Hodge cracked his eyes open to just a slit. By firelight he saw an object dangling from a golden chain.

"Thank you for keeping it safe," Prince Leo said, reaching for the object.

Lord Pertwie snatched it back and laughed. "Perhaps I'll keep it still. It could come in useful."

"No," the prince said in a cold voice. "You will give it to me."

Lord Pertwie laughed again. "Of course. A small matter. Now, we must get busy." He left the tent with Prince Leo limping on a crutch behind him.

Hodge burned inside, but not with fever. Though his wound kept him bound to the cot, his mind raged about the tent, hurling itself at everything within his vision. "You lied to me," he cried, clinching his eyes shut against tears of anger and frustration. Though there was no one there to hear, he railed at the impossibility of his situation.

By the time Prince Leo returned, Hodge had worn himself out. He could only glare.

"Ah," said the prince. "You are awake. The sun has risen on a beautiful day."

Hodge said nothing.

"I feared for your life. It is well we got you here, though I hesitated at first, remembering your last encounter with Lord Pertwie. His surgeon has done an admirable job. You should be up and about in a few days. But for now you must rest. Perhaps soon you'll be fit enough for a game of chess. What do you say?"

"Where is Jayne?"

"She is fine."

"I want to see her."

The prince laughed. "Yes, I don't blame you. Such a lovely girl."

Hodge's heart caught at those words—an intermingling of tenderness and fear. The tenderness surprised him.

"What have you done with her?"

The prince drew back in surprise. "Why, nothing. She is perfectly safe with Cull. He would not let any harm befall her. Though a bit coarse, he is a good man."

Hodge grunted at that.

Prince Leo leaned his crutch against a tent pole and sat

on the camp stool next to Hodge's cot. "You know, you told me so much of the wonders of that cave of yours. It's too bad you never had a chance to show me. Maybe someday."

"You lied to me."

"I saved your life."

"You said the king's army would be here. That Fleet would be here. You *are* a traitor, just like they said."

"There are reasons for everything."

"You are as evil as Lord Pertwie."

"Maybe so, but he would have let you die."

"You're a worthy pair."

"Perhaps we are."

CHAPTER TWENTY-THREE

*W*hen the surgeon came later that morning to tend
to Hodge, Jayne accompanied him. She watched
while the dressing was removed and the wound treated
with sphagnum moss and antiseptic herbs.

"It should heal well now," the surgeon said. "I believe
the fever is held at bay. Someone knew how to care for the
wound."

Hodge grimaced as a clean bandage was tied in place.

"There, that is done," the surgeon said. "I will return
this evening. Though not really necessary, His Highness
will insist."

After the surgeon left, Jayne took his place on the stool.
"*His Highness* said you could finally have some company."
She leaned forward and peered into Hodge's face. "How
are you feeling?"

Tears welled up in his eyes. "I'll never find Fleet. He might as well be dead."

Jayne took his hand. "You will find him." But the confidence was gone from her voice. She shook her head. "I was wrong when I said the prince didn't look like a traitor. Now I hate the sight of him."

"It's worse than that. He intends to attack the capital city, and there will be no armies there to defend it."

"What? Why not?"

"I heard the prince tell Lord Pertwie that the king's armies are gathering at . . . I don't remember where. My brain is such a muddle."

Jayne released his hand. "What good would it do if you did remember? We could never get there."

"Still, shouldn't the king be warned?"

"Is the king any better? Maybe they should all just kill one another, until none of them are left." Jayne's shoulders slumped. "At least that's what Bilda said when she found out my Tom was dead." She wiped at her eyes.

In the silence that followed, Hodge could hear the thrumming sounds of the camp around him—the sounds of preparation for war. A flood of awful memories washed over him: his shock at finding Castle Marlby nearly destroyed by Lord Pertwie's war machines; the horror of the battlefield and the grief within the castle walls; his aching to find Fleet. Yet all that time he had been caught at Prince Leo's side, as if he had no will of his own.

"No!" Hodge exclaimed. "We must do something. We can't leave the people to the mercy of Prince Leo and Lord Pertwie." He concentrated on the words that had passed between the two scoundrels, trying now to remember all that was said. "They plan on attacking Warnick while the king is at . . . at. . . ." He pounded his forehead with his fist.

Jayne pulled at his hand. "It won't help to beat yourself up."

"Ahhh! While the king is at . . . Kingsfort! Of course! I'm an idiot for not remembering. Whether the father be good or bad, the people shouldn't have to suffer the son. But how can we get there? Can the donkey take us in time?"

"Only a horse would be fast enough."

"I've never ridden before. I . . . I don't know how."

"I have ridden—a bit. But these are not plow horses."

"How different could they be? Are Cull and Wat still about?"

"Yes, but—"

"We'll need their help if we're to get a horse." Hodge ran his hand through his ragged hair. "I've no idea how to find Kingsfort."

"But your leg?"

"It doesn't matter. The surgeon said it will heal. And if I don't have to walk—" He pushed himself to a sitting

position. "See, I'm already much better." A different kind of fever burned through him at the thought of the task ahead. "We can do this. First you must find out where Kingsfort is. Ask around the camp, but take care. Tell Cull what we have planned. See if he and Wat can steal us a horse. The surgeon will be here to check on me before nightfall. Then we can escape under cover of darkness."

"But Hodge—"

"Jayne, I've never been good for anything but cleaning out ovens. From the time I was little I dreamed of serving royalty, like the kings in the stories Jesper told. But I don't think those kings exist. Now it's come to this, and I must do something. *We* must. There is no one else!"

Jayne bit her lip. "It won't be easy."

"Coming here wasn't easy either." Hodge took her hand again. "Jayne, I'm no hero, like in the stories. Maybe even those stories aren't true. This will be more like sneaking around and bearing tales than fighting great battles, but will you help me?"

Hodge held her eyes in his. She didn't try to look away. "Yes, of course I will."

"Thank you. It all depends on you now. You'll have to arrange everything. Can you manage?"

"I think so. Lord Pertwie had us guarded at first. I'm afraid I was a bit frantic when I discovered where we were. I kicked a soldier or two. But now we seem to be left

alone. As if we were of no account." Jayne stood up. "I'll find Cull and tell him what we are planning. He will help."

✦ ✦ ✦

The day crept along. At noon a bit of food and drink were brought in by a gnarled old man who smelled of ale and sweat. The ancient lackey stood swaying at the foot of the cot while Hodge ate, then he gathered the tray and cup and tottered off to other duties.

As the afternoon wore on, the sun beat down on the pavilion. Hodge squirmed beneath his borrowed nightshirt. He scanned the tent for his own clothes, but he couldn't see them anywhere—another thing to ask Jayne about when she returned.

He pushed back the restrictive bedcovers. The air felt cool on his hot and sticky legs. Though he had always fought Bilda on bath day, he wished he could have one now—or at least a dunk in the Eiderlee. He tried to remember what had become of the jeweled comb Prince Leo had given him so many ages ago. He wondered if the prince still had the stolen knife.

At last Jayne peeked into the tent.

"I thought you'd never get here," Hodge said. "What have you found?"

She hurried to Hodge's side. "I know how to find

Kingsfort. Northward through the wilderness we'll strike the High Road. Then east toward morning."

"Good! Did anyone seem suspicious with your asking?"

Jayne smiled. "Around the bustle of the cook fires I could have asked anything and not raised an eyebrow. It was easy enough to get my questions answered."

"What about a horse?"

"Cull and Wat will see to it. But not until after dark. It's too dangerous now."

"And my clothes?"

She glanced around. "Aren't they here?" She searched the tent, pushing aside blankets and bedding. "You can't go in just a nightshirt."

"I can if I need to, though boots would be nice."

"Don't worry, I'll find you something. I'll come back after dark. We'll wait for Cull. Now I must go. Get some rest and be ready."

"How can I do both?"

But she was already gone.

✦ ✦ ✦

When the surgeon came to replace the bandages, he insisted that Hodge cover up. "You don't want to let the bad air into your wound," he said. "And the blankets will keep away the chill."

But Hodge couldn't feel any sign of a chill in the air, so as soon as the surgeon left, he kicked the blankets off. Though afternoon light still shone at the tent door, darkness invaded the far corners of the tent. By the time dinner was brought in by the same foul-smelling lackey, Hodge could barely make out what was on the tray. It turned out to be dark bread and some sort of cheese—a richer, nuttier cheese than he had ever tasted before—and wine.

While he was eating, Prince Leo entered with a lantern. He dismissed the lackey.

"A little light," he said, "to go with that fine cheese and wine. Pertwie may be a scoundrel, but at least he keeps a respectable table. How do you like it?"

Go away, Hodge thought.

The prince sat on the stool, tilting to one side as if he were a little drunk. "Of all the great feasts I've attended, just being huddled up with a bit of bread and cheese is what I've enjoyed the most. With wine of course. Lots of wine." He laughed and poured himself a cup. "Yes, lots of wine."

Hodge glanced out the entrance. The sunlight was rapidly fading. Jayne would soon return. He grunted at the prince. "It tastes all right."

"Come, how about a game of chess? With all the flurry of preparation, no one seems willing to oblige me."

"Preparation for what?"

"Oh, a little scheme Lord Pertwie has hatched. Now, will you indulge me? One game?"

"No. I . . . I've forgotten how."

The prince withdrew the cup from his mouth without taking a drink. "You are angry."

Unwilling to return the prince's gaze, Hodge stared out the tent door into the growing night. He almost choked when Jayne appeared. She stepped inside before realizing the prince was there.

"Oh!"

"Come in, come in," Prince Leo said. "Join us. I was just trying to talk Lord Hodge into a game of chess. You may cheer on the winner."

Jayne stammered for a moment. She shifted the bag she carried to behind her back. "I . . . I just came to check on Hodge, to see how he's getting on." With a quick glance out the doorway she moved closer to the cot. "It's getting late," she said with a meaningful nod.

Prince Leo slapped his thigh. "Nonsense. The night is young, and so are we. There is yet time." He drained the cup he had poured for himself. "Sing us a song, Jayne Kemp." He staggered to his feet and bowed. "Pardon me— *Lady* Jayne Kemp. Sing us a song."

"But Your Highness, I'm no singer. Perhaps around the campfires you might find better entertainment."

"Oh, ho! You're trying to get rid of me."

"No—"

"Yes. You want Lord Hodge to yourself. Well, that I understand. Such a fine young man he is. So handsome and regal. But a young couple needs a chaperone. I feel duty-bound to remain."

In spite of his anxiety, Hodge blushed at the thought of himself and Jayne as a couple. He glanced at her.

"We need no chaperone," she said.

A gruff voice called from outside the tent, "Hey now, are ye set?" Cull ducked through the entrance. "Are ye ready?" He froze upon seeing Prince Leo. "What's *he* doin' here?"

The prince cast a suspicious look at Cull, then Jayne. "What's going on?"

Cull barged across the floor and felled the prince with a single bone-cracking blow.

"Let's be hurrying. If he ain't dead, he'll be waking soon. Best tie him up and stuff his mouth. That'll give us 'til mornin'."

"Wait," Hodge said. He hobbled to the inert body. "This could come in useful." He pulled the golden chain from around the prince's neck and put it around his own, hiding the royal seal beneath his nightshirt.

CHAPTER TWENTY-FOUR

*C*ull carried Hodge through the camp with Jayne hurrying along beside him. In the midst of all the battle preparations, no one paid them much heed. Sometimes it was useful to be of no significance, Hodge thought.

"They be a might confident in their position," whispered Cull. "To our advantage."

Wat awaited them within a copse of trees just beyond the last reaches of firelight. He led them to the horse. As Jayne had feared, it was no mere plow animal, but rather a silvery gray giant whose ear-shattering cry could have disturbed the dead in far-off Araby.

Wat stroked the stallion's neck to settle him. "Hush now, ye big lummox."

The horse shook his head, sweeping his mane about as

if eager for action. Cull set Hodge, still in his nightshirt, upon the animal's broad back. Then he helped Jayne to her place in front of Hodge.

"A saddle for this monster would have been too chancy." He handed Hodge the bag of supplies. "You'll have to ride bareback. Just let him know who his master is—with a club if need be." He gave the reins to Jayne. "He's a warhorse, keen to the scent of blood, so it'll take a tight hand to keep him to task. Now be off. Straightway through the forest." He pointed above the trees at the brightly glimmering North Star. "Keep to *her*. And pray for a clear night."

"But what about my clothes?" Hodge asked.

"There's no time for that." Cull slapped the horse's flank. The animal leaped forward through the shadows. Hodge had trouble keeping his rear on the back of the horse. He had no chance to wave good-bye.

"Hold on to me," Jayne said.

He wrapped his arms about her waist. "Do you . . . do you think we'll be followed?" Each heaving stride sent a stab of pain through his leg.

"I pray not. The camp was a noisy enough place. By the time they find the prince, we'll be well beyond their reach."

Her hair flew into Hodge's face, tickling his nose. It seemed to him like they raced through the forest for a good long while. Finally Jayne pulled on the reins, tugging back with all her weight against him. The horse's thudding stride slowed to a walk.

"Cull was right," Jayne said, breathing heavily. "A tight hand. But we don't want to run him all night."

Hodge relaxed. This pace was much easier on his leg. As the horse lumbered through the woods, Hodge was reminded of a time long ago when he and Fleet had ridden upon the broad, rolling back of a cow. It was when they were only boys—before Fleet had become so busy with the falcons. The two had wandered far afoot, across the meadows beyond the village, hunting wild strawberries. Too lazy to walk back to the castle on their own, they had commandeered a cow. But she had a mind of her own, and their enthusiastic prodding only took them farther afield. Now, it seemed this giant warhorse had already carried Hodge beyond the edge of the world.

After a bit, he became restless. He squirmed about, trying to find a comfortable spot for his injured leg. Jayne pulled the horse to a stop.

"You should get dressed now. It's getting cold."

She helped him from the horse's high back and pulled a set of clothes from the bag. "The boots may be overlarge," she said. "But they'll do."

Hodge felt their supple leather in his fingers. He had never worn anything so fine. "Where did you get them?"

"They're Prince Leo's, I think, provided him by Lord Pertwie, as are the tunic and hose."

"I can't wear these things!"

"Yes, you can." She held the embroidered tunic up to measure against him. "The shoulders are broad enough, and the back plenty stout. They'll fit you."

"No. They're too grand. I could never wear them."

"You must wear something, else you'll get ill all over again. Here, take them. Hurry. We must be on our way."

For a fleeting moment Jayne's businesslike air reminded him of Bilda—so different from the frightened girl of several days ago. All reservations of yesterday were gone, and she seemed as intent on this adventure as he.

He took the clothes. He was surprised at how comfortable the soft fabric felt against his skin. He pulled on the tunic and the hose—not wool, but silk.

"Are you ready?" Jayne had averted her eyes while he dressed, busying herself with the horse.

"Just about." He sat on a fallen log and tugged at the boots. They were a bit narrow, but they fit well enough. He arose. Though his leg still ached, the clothes made him want to stand as tall as he was able. "How do I look?"

Jayne turned about. She laughed. "You're only lacking a bonnet to look like a prince."

He tried to keep his shrug nonchalant. He knew she was just being kind, but even so he felt a blush starting.

"We'd better move on, now," Jayne said. "Morning will be upon us soon enough."

She helped Hodge climb upon the horse's back. "You ride in front. You can stretch your leg out along his neck. It will be more comfortable."

Hodge obeyed by sliding forward to the animal's shoulder. Then he offered Jayne his hand, and she climbed up behind him. He was immediately conscious of her arms reaching around to take the reins. He felt a nervous warmth stealing through him.

He tried to turn his mind to other things. "Do you suppose Fleet is all right?"

"I'm certain of it. He's waiting for us, there with the king's army. You'll see him tomorrow."

Hodge nodded, grateful to hear the hope returning to Jayne's voice. It made him yearn to lean back into her reassuring presence. "It's my fault he's gone, you know. I wouldn't listen to him. He warned me, but I was blinded by the prince."

Jayne was quiet for a moment. "There are many things that can blind you," she finally said.

They continued their ride through the night. Occasionally Jayne would hurry the horse to a trot, but no faster. "If he gets away from me," she said, "I'm afraid he'll take us past the end of the earth before I can stop him."

Hodge remembered the feeling he had had earlier and

wondered if Jayne had read his thoughts. Exhaustion pulled at him again. Surely he must have rested enough, but his body still felt weak, as if he were standing between two worlds—this one and another he couldn't quite identify.

He opened the bag he carried before him. "Are you hungry?" he asked.

"I'm fair famished."

He handed back a bit of dry biscuit he had ferreted from the sack. "There's more—mostly broken pieces and crumbs. And water."

"Thank you."

He peeked around her, back along the way they had come. Morning light crept through the trees.

"This horse leaves a heavy track," he said. He could easily make out the trampled swath that marked their passage through the undergrowth. "Lord Pertwie's men would have no trouble—" He stopped with a gulp.

"What?"

"We're being followed!" He had caught the distant sight of two mounted riders galloping toward them through the trees.

Jayne glanced back, then slapped the reins and kicked with her heels. Their mount lumbered to a trot. She kicked harder. The horse shifted to a canter.

"Faster," Hodge cried.

Jayne continued her frantic efforts. The horse picked up

more speed. Hodge glimpsed the pursuing riders dodging through the trees, gaining with each passing moment.

"Faster!"

"I'm trying!"

Gradually the giant horse gathered momentum, until he too was galloping headlong through the forest. Hodge stole another look back. The riders were within fifty yards, but they were no longer closing the distance.

It felt as if the horse were flying, his hooves barely touching the ground. He took as straight a line as possible, exploding through the undergrowth, leaping fallen logs, passing perilously close to the outstretched trees.

"We're outrunning them," Jayne said between gasps of breath.

Hodge felt branches slap against his face, and then they burst out of the forest into open daylight. The ground below them sloped toward a stone-paved highway.

"The High Road," Jayne cried. She hauled on the reins. Sparks flew as hooves at last struck the paving stones.

The pursuing riders stopped at the edge of the wood. One raised a bow and took careful aim.

"Look out!" Hodge cried.

Jayne swerved the horse, and the speeding arrow buried itself harmlessly in the grass beyond the road. "Are they following?" she asked.

"Not in the open. They must be wary of the road."

Jayne kicked her heels again. "They'll not be able to keep up. They'll be fighting the forest."

"How much farther is it?"

"Half a day along the road. That's what the cooks said."

"But we can't run him 'til then, can we?"

"I expect even he'll need rest. But so will our pursuers."

Hodge had a sudden thought. "Jayne? What do you suppose has happened to Cull and Wat?"

"I . . ." Her voice faltered.

"If we're being followed," Hodge said, "they must have been discovered."

Jayne said nothing.

"And if they were discovered," Hodge said, "they're likely . . ." He dared not finish the thought.

Still Jayne did not speak.

Hodge gritted his teeth. "If that be the case," he said, "I will kill Prince Leo myself."

CHAPTER TWENTY-FIVE

*I*t must have been the sweeping turn of the road that allowed the riders to get ahead of Hodge and Jayne. The pursuers raced out from under the trees at an intercepting angle. At least their speed made it impossible for them to nock an arrow.

"Faster," Hodge cried.

Jayne slapped the reins and leaned into Hodge. The horse's breath came in fearsome bursts, yet his heaving body continued strong and sure. It appeared for a moment they would surge past the pursuit, but the stallion stumbled on a broken paving stone. With heroic effort he managed to keep his riders from falling by lurching forward on his knees. His cry split the air as he clambered back to all fours. But it was too late. The men had cut them off.

"Hold or I'll shoot." Even on his skittering horse, the first already had an arrow trained on them at close range. The second circled about and cut off their escape to the rear.

Jayne tried to keep their horse still, but he seemed to sense a danger he had been trained for. He muscled sideways toward the archer, shouldering into the man's mount.

"I'll shoot," the man yelled, trying to back away.

Seeing his chance, Hodge grabbed the arrow and wrenched it from the bow. Their stallion reared and exploded past the rider. The man let out an angry cry as he fell. The other cursed, and Hodge heard the slither of metal on leather.

"Watch out!" he cried.

A sword whistled and thudded into something as they lunged past the second rider.

Jayne looked to the road ahead, keeping the horse at a full run. Hodge craned his neck to watch behind. Once remounted, the enemy riders started in pursuit, but then seemed to think better of it and turned back toward the trees.

"They're giving up," Hodge said.

"Good," Jayne answered, "because something's wrong with our horse."

"What?"

"Can't you feel it?"

Hodge noticed the uneven stride, barely perceptible as they raced along the road.

"He's hurt," Jayne said, glancing back. "He's bleeding."

A coppery sheen covered the straining muscles of the animal's haunch, but still he labored on. Jayne reined the horse in and slid off his back.

Hodge searched the road behind. The enemy riders were nowhere to be seen. "Have they really given up?" he asked, dropping heavily to the ground.

"I don't know. They could come out of the forest anywhere. Did they see his wound?"

"How bad is it?"

"The cut is deep." She dabbed at it with her cloak. "I don't think I can stop the bleeding. We shouldn't be riding him. He shouldn't even be walking."

"And we shouldn't keep to the road. Those men might return." Hodge shielded his eyes from the morning sun and looked across the highway. "Maybe we can travel hidden in the woods. And find a place where the horse will be safe." He turned to Jayne. "We have no choice now but to go afoot."

"What about your leg?"

He shook his head. "My leg will have to do."

They set off into the woods with Jayne leading the animal. Hodge limped along beside the horse. Before long they found a shaded spot where the grass was plentiful and a spring bubbled up to form a small pool amongst ferns and mosses.

"This will do," Jayne said.

Hodge sank to the ground. Already his leg throbbed with each beat of his heart. He thought it might be pleasant to rest here for a while.

The horse buried his nose in the water.

"Will he be all right?" Hodge asked.

"He's strong, and smart enough."

"He saved us, you know."

"I know."

"Where did Cull find him?"

"For aught I know, this was Lord Pertwie's mount. He's certainly a nobleman's steed."

Hodge laughed. "Me in Prince Leo's clothes, on Lord Pertwie's warhorse! That'll be a tale to share with Fleet. He'll not believe it." Hodge rose and slung their bag over his shoulder. "We best be on our way. If we keep within sight of the road, we should manage well enough." He searched through the undergrowth and found a weather-worn branch that would serve as a walking stick. He also made sure their water skin was filled.

"Ready?"

Jayne stroked the horse's neck and whispered a good-bye. Then she and Hodge set off on foot through the woods.

They hadn't gone but fifty yards before they became aware of a plodding noise behind them.

"Oh, dear," Jayne said.

The horse had followed, limping in his attempt to catch up to them. Jayne took the reins and led him back to the spring. She hurried to rejoin Hodge, but the stallion followed her again.

"Go back!" Jayne cried.

"Can't we just tie him up there?" Hodge asked.

"That would be cruel. Who would come to free him after we've gone?"

"But what else can we do?"

Jayne sighed. "Nothing. I'll never stop him if he's made up his mind to follow."

"Maybe he'll tire and won't be able to keep up."

"Maybe."

For the rest of the morning Hodge and Jayne crept through the thick forest with a giant warhorse lumbering along behind.

CHAPTER TWENTY-SIX

I need to rest," Hodge said.

He had gone as far as he was able, then he gritted his teeth and struggled on for another hour. But now he was utterly spent. He lowered himself to a fallen log. Blood had seeped through his bandage to stain the upper leg of his hose.

The horse stood close by with his head drooping toward the ground.

Hodge patted his neck. "Here, Bert. You'll be all right."

"Bert?" Jayne asked.

"He needs a name, don't he? And he makes a better Bert than Bert the ostler."

Jayne laughed. Hodge wished she would keep on laughing. He loved the ringing sound of it, but they hadn't had much to be merry about the last few days.

"Yes, he does," Jayne said. "But I'm afraid this Bert's fair worn out."

Hodge's own tired muscles agreed. "He is. We can rest here for a short while."

But he hadn't counted on how much the day's exhaustion had piled on them. Jayne fell asleep first, curled up in her cloak in the shade of a birch tree. Hodge thought briefly how pleasant it would be to rest before the fire in the Great Hall. But before he could imagine the snap and crackle of the roaring blaze he, too, was fast asleep.

✦ ✦ ✦

"Hodge, wake up."

"Leave me alone."

"Please, wake up."

Hodge turned away from the gentle shaking. "What for?"

"Shhhh."

He turned his voice to a whisper. "What for?" He tried to hunker back down into his nap.

"Bert's heard something."

Hodge winced at the old name, but then remembered its more recent connection. He sat up and looked about. "Where?"

"I can't tell," Jayne said. "I've not got his ears."

The horse stood erect and as still as if he had turned to

marble while they slept. He nickered in the back of his throat.

Hodge clambered to his feet. "What is it?"

"Shhh. Listen. Can't you hear it now?"

"I've not got *your* ears. I can't— Wait, there it is. From the road."

The sound fluttered in the late afternoon warmth, at first a musical tinkling, barely perceptible above the breeze. Then came a jangling rattle, followed by the clashing of metal on metal. After a few moments the clopping of horses' hooves became audible, adding a steady rhythm to the chorus. At last the heavy rumble of carts and wagons churned the sounds into a plodding, driving movement.

Keeping himself hidden, Hodge crept forward to peer from the trees. A whole army was passing below them on the High Road, pale-blue banners flapping throughout their ranks. Horses strutted, proudly carrying their armored riders. Grim footmen followed with pikes polished and flashing sharply in the sun. Supply wagons rolled along the road and horse carts with their attendant lackeys spread out on either side, nearly filling the whole valley with their passage.

"What army is it?" Jayne asked.

Hodge hesitated to say. For all appearances this multitude was heading to Kingsfort to join the royal muster, but still they seemed no different than the forces that bore the silver and green under Lord Pertwie's command. Like those, these soldiers carried themselves with the same rigid sense of purpose: hard of eye, firm of jaw, their gaze intent on some objective that lay in the distance before them.

"Maybe we should join them," Jayne said.

"I don't think we could keep up."

"Maybe they would—"

"Make no sound," growled a voice from behind.

Hodge spun about.

"No, nor move neither," said another.

Hodge froze at the glint of steel-tipped arrows.

"We should kill them now, before they raise the alarm," said the first man. "That's Roland's army that passes yonder. I'm not one to be left dawdling with them about."

"Our orders were clear. No harm to the boy."

"That may not be of our choosing," said the first. "At all costs we must keep these two from reaching the king—and keep ourselves healthy and hale to boot."

Though the men spoke in quiet tones, as if they were discussing a bit of gossip over a mug of ale, neither took his eyes off his target. Hodge felt an overwhelming urge to bolt toward the army on the road. With great effort he held himself in check, though he feared his body might act of its own accord.

The stallion stepped toward the men.

"Watch that beast!"

"We needn't spare the horse. I could put an arrow in his eye before he could blink."

"Not with Roland down below. I'll not chance the noise." The man nodded at Hodge. "You, boy. Away from that animal."

Hodge obeyed, one eye fixed steadily on the men, the other on the horse. He had sensed the tremor of impatience that rippled across Bert's flank. The horse took another step. Both arrows swung toward him. With an ear-splitting bellow he leaped at the nearest man. Bowstrings thrummed. The horse stumbled and fell, crashing into the archer. His full weight smashed down onto the man, forcing a strangled cry from his throat. Hodge snatched up a fist-sized stone and hurled it at the other, striking him in the face before he could nock a second arrow. Another rock, thrown from Jayne's side of the clearing, dropped him to the ground.

Then, all was quiet except for the rolling echo of the army's passage.

PART IV

The World's End

The greatest of all these.

CHAPTER TWENTY-SEVEN

*H*odge and Jayne stood in the middle of the road and watched as the last of the wagons rumbled into the distance. A thick cloud still hung in the air, churned up by horses and heavy wheels. The settling dust clung to Jayne's tear-stained face.

"I killed him," she said between sniffling gasps. "That man. I killed him."

Hodge nodded. "*We* killed him."

Her lip trembled as she struggled to stop the tears. "And poor Bert."

Hodge glanced back at the trees. He nodded again and thought of everyone who had come to grief because of him. All because he had allowed Prince Leo, eldest son of his Royal Majesty, King Alfred the Second, and heir presumptive to the throne, to steal his knife. The memory of it weighed down his heart. He tried to think of something that would divert both their minds.

"Do you remember last harvest time?" he asked. It seemed so long ago, ages past, when he was still a boy. "Bilda's feast was the finest ever. There were baked apples and roasted squash with pork stuffing and snap-cider and grapes that smelled like winter coming."

Jayne sniffled in response.

"Do you remember the mummers that came to the keep?" Hodge continued. "Do you remember the comedy they played? About the Tinker's shrewish wife who died but was too stubborn to lay her body down? She kept nagging her poor husband until her tongue dropped out of her head and her teeth fell out and her skin rotted away. And still she followed him about on bony feet, wagging her bony finger in his face."

Jayne smiled through her tears. Hodge was distracted by the sparkle it brought to her eyes.

"Well, that's me," he said, trying to re-collect his thoughts. "I'm too stubborn to lay my body down. Though I'll try not to be such a complainer." He settled the bag on his shoulder. He rubbed at the pain in his thigh and looked after the vanished army. "Lord Roland's forces are for the king. I heard Lord Pertwie say. Maybe if we catch them, they'll take us to the king."

"And there perhaps we will find your brother."

Hodge frowned. The idea that her words might be true seemed like a hand-grasp in the freezing cold—numb and unsure.

◆ ◆ ◆

As they continued their trek, Hodge's limping walk turned into a painful hobble, though as promised, he didn't complain, even when it became obvious they would never catch Lord Roland's army. When the ache grew too great to bear he thought of Bert the warhorse and his well-trained sense of duty. Or of Cull and his unselfish assistance to strangers. Or further back to Fleet and his endless patience with a foolish brother. With those memories strengthening him, Hodge was able to continue through the pain. It seemed Jayne sensed those times. More than once she offered her arm for support.

He couldn't tell whether she moved slowly for his sake or because of her own exhaustion, but he was grateful when she finally said, "It's getting dark, we should rest."

He gratefully sank to the ground. In the morning, he awoke to daylight and a painful stiffness. "Jayne, it's time to move on."

She sat up to pull her cloak about herself. Hodge noticed more tears.

"What's wrong?" he asked.

She shook her head. "Nothing." She avoided Hodge's eyes. "I was just remembering."

"Tom?"

She nodded. "And Bilda and Martin's Mary and Lord Selden. And Castle Marlby. There's nowhere for us now."

Hodge knew what she meant. Their home at Castle Marlby seemed a place of ancient happiness, buried beneath the rubble of a thousand years. There would be no returning to the tranquil life they had known. And ahead, beyond Kingsfort, the future was lost in a cloud.

Hodge picked up his walking stick and their bag of dwindling provisions. "Come on," he said, more cheerfully than he felt. "We've had a good night's rest. If we hurry, we should arrive in time for the noonday meal."

They set out into the late summer morning. A hint of autumn hung in the air: the distant smell of moldering leaves and yellowed grasses. Hodge thought again of harvest time.

"Your limp is getting worse," Jayne said after a while.

He grimaced at her reminder. "Only a bit. It can't be much farther."

"If the fever takes you, I will have no one left."

"I'll be all right." He spoke the words, but they seemed a lie. It took nearly all his wit to move himself forward. He didn't have much left for dishonesty.

Soon the road began a climb into the hills. Hodge

looked upward and faltered. The sight drained what little strength he had left.

"You need to rest," Jayne said.

"No. We must keep going. If I stop now, I'll not get up again."

"But, Hodge—"

"Please. We're running out of time. I've slowed us down enough."

Jayne offered her arm. "Lean on me, then."

She supported his weight and together they trudged upward. Hodge's eyes focused on the cobbled road at his feet, and he concentrated on putting one foot before the other. To distract himself he counted the paving stones in his mind. He had decided how many would be left until the summit, but when he arrived at that number, the top seemed no closer than before. He looked toward the pass. It lay hidden beyond the curve of the road.

He chose another number and began again. He didn't realize that this time he was speaking aloud.

"What are you doing?" Jayne asked.

"Uh, counting. Twelve . . . thirteen . . . fourteen . . ."

"Counting what?"

"Stones—fifteen . . . sixteen . . . seventeen . . ."

"What for?

"To see how many there are—twenty-three . . . twenty-four . . . twenty-five . . ."

Twenty-six never left his mouth. It was interrupted by a shouted command.

"Halt!"

Armed men seemed to spring out of the ground to surround the two travelers.

"What business have ye in Kingsfort?"

Hodge forgot his counting and sank to the ground, giving in to exhaustion. "The king," he cried in relief, "we have news for the king."

Jayne knelt beside him, still clutching his arm. "We've come a long way," she said. "And my friend is hurt."

A young knight leaped forward, his mail coat rattling in his hurry. "He *is* injured, Sir," he called to his captain, "his back and leg."

Hodge shook his head. "It's just my leg."

The captain stooped before them. "What news for the king?"

Hodge pulled the chain from around his neck and held up the royal seal. "News of Prince Leo."

✦ ✦ ✦

In a blur of motion, Hodge found himself and Jayne in the back of a horse-drawn cart, bouncing along the road with the young knight, Sir Collen, galloping beside them.

"Hodge, look," Jayne said, kneeling at the front of the cart. "Kingsfort!"

She helped him rise up high enough to look out across the wide valley. His eyes grew wide with amazement. Prince Leo had been right: He and Lord Pertwie would never have been victorious against such an army. The land around Kingsfort was filled with a sprawling city of tents and banners and battle flags. In the center of the plain a single stone tower rose above the innumerable pavilions. The midday sun shone down on the yellow and red banners that flew from the tower's parapets. It was toward this imposing edifice that Hodge and Jayne were carried. Every sentry challenge along the way was met by a raised hand from Sir Collen and a hurried conversation, after which they were allowed to continue with redoubled speed.

As they approached the raised earth motte on which the tower stood, however, the crowds grew thicker, and their passage slowed. They drew many curious stares, but Sir Collen pushed ahead to the wall that surrounded the tower motte. The sentries at the barbican gate parted to let them through without a challenge.

"We're here," Jayne whispered, as if she were afraid the sound of her voice would dissolve it all away. "Your brother may be close at hand."

Hodge nodded, though his stomach knotted. He vacillated between fear that Fleet would not be found and nervousness at how he would greet his brother.

Sir Collen helped Hodge out of the cart and led him and Jayne inside a well-appointed pavilion. "You must tell your news to His Lord, the High Chamberlain," Sir Collen said. "He will decide what is to be done."

"My Lord," he said, addressing a man who sat behind a great oak table spread with books and parchments. "Word of Prince Leo."

The man looked up and removed the spectacles that clung to the end of his nose. "Yes," he said in a high, wheezing voice. "Proceed."

Another man stepped out of the shadows—a wizened old soldier in carmine robes trimmed with fox, beneath which glinted the blue metal of a mail shirt. "Ah," he said. "Word of Prince Leo. So he's not dead as was reported."

Hodge held forth the royal seal. "No." But then he remembered Cull's jarring blow that had left the prince senseless. "Leastwise I don't think so."

The High Chamberlain leaned forward. "His father will be glad," he said. "But you have also brought a warning?"

Hodge nodded. "Yes. Prince Leo and Lord Pertwie don't intend to meet your armies in battle. Their plan is to attack Warnick directly."

The old soldier came forward and took the seal from Hodge's hand. He nodded as he examined it. "Indeed. Please, tell us how you came by this information."

Trying not to jumble his words, Hodge related the story from the very beginning. He told them everything except for the bewildering attachment he had begun to feel for Jayne Kemp.

"Cowards," growled the old soldier. "Leo and Pertwie are cowards."

"Yes, Sir Champhries," the Chamberlain said with a nod. "But they are right. A strike at Warnick would be devastating. There is no time to lose."

In a swirl of cloaks the two men disappeared through hanging curtains at the rear of the tent.

"Your duty is performed," Sir Collen said. "Now we may see to your healing."

Hodge turned about to face him. "No, not yet. I must find my brother. He was at Castle Marlby during the siege. He joined the king's armies there. I must find him."

"Ah, yes, the Marlby contingent. They fought bravely. They are close at hand. I will take you to them. And on the way we will find a surgeon to re-dress your wound, Sir Hodge."

Hodge started at the title. He remembered the prince's mocking address. "I'm not a knight."

"But your clothes? Surely these are the vestments of a noble."

He lowered his head. "I am Hodge, son of Rolf the fletcher. These clothes were borrowed so I could escape in more than just my nightshirt. I am nobody."

Sir Collen smiled. "You are nobody? Just a young man who worked his way into Prince Leo's confidence, detected Lord Pertwie's treachery, and against all odds escaped to bring us word that may save the kingdom. Is that who you are?"

Hodge blushed. "I—I had help."

CHAPTER TWENTY-EIGHT

Sir Collen located a surgeon within the tower bailey
and pressed him into service. The surgeon gathered
up a few bottles and jars, several knives, and a saw, and
placed them in a leather satchel. They proceeded through
the gate of the tower motte and along its outer wall.
Hodge's stomach turned nearly inside out with anticipation. He feared he would squeeze Jayne's hand to pieces.

"It's all right," she said, trying to calm him. "Soon we'll
know."

A jumble of tents had been erected near the pavilions
of the king's own army. They seemed to be part of that
larger force, though separate, too, as if they didn't quite fit
in. At last Hodge saw a face he recognized.

"Sir Granby," he cried. "It's me, Hodge. And Jayne
Kemp, too."

The old captain-of-the-guard looked up from the bubbling stewpot near which he squatted. A purple welt ran across the bridge of his nose and down his cheek, but his eyes were bright and alert. He rose to his feet.

"Hodge. And Jayne Kemp." A smile spread across his face. "How now? What news of Castle Marlby?"

"The keep is damaged sore," Hodge said, "and the people scattered. But some are returning. And you? Who is with you here?" He hesitated to ask the question that burned in his mind.

Sir Granby indicated the men who sat about with him. "Here's Sir William and Henry. And you remember Brock, the youngest of Sir Robert Carville. There's a few others left with us, but they are out and about today."

Hodge looked around at the old familiar faces. It was good to see them there, smiling back at him. "And—and my brother, Fleet?" he asked. "Where is he?"

The smiles faded. Sir Granby placed a hand on Hodge's shoulder. "Fleet's not here."

"Then where is he?"

Sir Granby pulled him around to look directly into his face. "Hodge, he never made it beyond the siege of Marlby. He was not trained for battle. I tried to dissuade him, but his heart was full of finding you. I fear we lost him on our own fields."

"Oh, Hodge," Jayne whispered.

He pulled away. "Did you . . . do you know of a surety

that he's . . . he's . . ." He couldn't bring himself to say the words.

"No, Hodge, I don't know of a surety that he's dead. The field was all blood and smoke and confusion. We were routed by the enemy and would still be flying, but for the appearance of Lord Roland. Many brave men fell, Hodge. Only a miracle could have saved your brother. And if it had, don't you think he would be with us now?"

Hodge felt a numbness creeping into his brain, a disbelief in what he heard—in everything that had happened through the last long weeks.

"Hodge," said a man who had come to stand next to Sir Collen. It was the High Chamberlain. "The king desires an audience with you."

✦ ✦ ✦

Sir Collen waited at the doorway while Hodge sat in the king's chamber. The surgeon had come along and now tended Hodge's wound, peeling off the bloodstained hose and cutting through the clotted bandages. Hodge barely noticed. His mind was still all tumbled about with Sir Granby's news. He wanted to get away, to be alone. His heart felt about to burst within his chest, but the private room of King Alfred was not the place to let grief have its way.

The king's chamber was high within the tower and

sparsely furnished with a simple slatted bed and a plain oak chair. Hodge sat on the only other furniture—a low bench—while the surgeon finished bandaging his leg. The clean linen seemed to ease the pain of his injury. Sir Collen handed him a new pair of leggings.

"Now take care of this wound," insisted the surgeon. "Too many people have been doctoring it for you to let it all go to naught."

Everything has already been for naught, Hodge thought. His unwarranted trust of Prince Leo, his decision to quit Castle Marlby, his journey to find Fleet—they had all been wasted. He wished these people would leave him alone now and let him go back home to whatever might be left. The king had no business interfering with his sorrow. Hodge had had enough of royalty to last the rest of his life. Perhaps, as Bilda had said, it would be better if the nobles just went away and left the common people to their own devices. As the thought worked its way through his mind, an old man entered the room. At his appearance Sir Collen bowed and backed out the doorway. The surgeon gathered up his implements and followed.

The old man lowered himself into the oak chair, slowly, as if his joints were stiff and uncooperative. "So, this is Hodge," he said in a quiet voice. "The young man who saved my son."

Still seated, Hodge stared at the old man. All this time

he had imagined King Alfred to be a broad-shouldered giant with a mane of snow-white hair flowing from beneath a golden crown. The figure who sat before him now was thin and shrunken. His robes hung on him, and though his hair was white, it wisped about in gossamer strands, shining like a halo in the dim candlelight. A thin, scraggly beard waggled from his chin as he talked. He wore no crown.

"When you left my son, how was he?" the king asked.

Hodge looked into the old, careworn face. The royal eyes glistened.

Hodge's own grief was too close to bear. He had to look away. "We left him well enough," he said.

"Tell me, how did he fare at Castle Marlby? Was he happy there?"

"He—he taught me to play chess."

"Ah. But for the joust, a favorite game of his. He played for hours on end with his brother, the young prince. Never could best him." The king coughed into a woolen scarf he wore about his neck. "And what about his comforts? Was he well-housed? Well-fed?"

"He ate well. I served his meals. And Bilda is the best cook in all the world."

"Good, good." King Alfred stood. With his hands behind his back, he paced the floor, his knobby knees creaking with every shuffling step he took. "Poor Leo. He just hasn't been the same since his brother died. All the wrong friends. All the wrong ideas."

The words struck hard at Hodge's own feeling. "His brother died?" He vaguely remembered asking the prince about a brother—or was that some muddled memory of Fleet?

The king stopped pacing. "Yes. A trifling wound from the practice field, gone to fever." He looked again at Hodge. "But now, my boy, you've come a long way to bring me news of my son. As a father, I am grateful. As your king, I am in your debt. Tell me, what can I do for you?"

This old man was not what Hodge had imagined a king to be. There was no air of arrogance about him, no condescending attitude. It reminded him of how Prince Leo treated him at Castle Marlby, but with no artifice about it.

"Your Highness?"

"You served my son well, and you have honorably served your king. I would repay your loyalty."

Hodge could no longer contain his grief. Tears sprang to his eyes and a shuddering sob burst from his tired body. In an instant the king was at his side.

"There, there, son. It's all right. It will be all right."

Hodge tried to speak, but the words were lost somewhere between the sobs and his gasps for air. Unable to stop himself, he fell into the arms of the old king and wept. He felt helpless and small—worn out by both hope and despair. King Alfred's kind hand on his back seemed to draw the tears from him in a never-ending flood.

A voice at the door said, "Your Highness, we must hurry."

"There is time enough," the king answered.

Hodge pulled away. "Your Highness," he said, "they . . . they're right."

"Nonsense. A few moments will not matter. My captains will have everything readied."

Hodge took a deep, shuddering breath and tried to gather his emotions back under control. "I'll be all right now," he said. "I . . . I'm sorry for—"

The king waved him to silence. "No, *I* am sorry. It was selfish of me—hauling you in here only to find news of my son. It's clear you have a grief of your own to bear. But now, if you do feel up to it, come. Perhaps action will allay both our sorrows. We do have a kingdom to save."

Hodge wiped his nose on his sleeve. "Yes, Your Highness."

The king arose. "Geoffrey, my armor."

A man, older even than the king, appeared out of nowhere to help His Majesty out of his robes. Without his clothes, the king looked like a scarecrow, all skinny arms and legs sticking out at odd angles from his loose-fitting undergarments. Several young pages entered, and layer by layer King Alfred was arrayed in his battle gear. First he was dressed in a woolen shirt, linen pants, and thick hose. Next a padded tunic was pulled over his head. The pages helped him into the mail chausses that would protect his legs. With great effort, the king wriggled into his hauberk, then the chain-mail coif which fit over his head like a woman's scarf. Over all was placed a red and yellow surcoat, emblazoned with his dragon coat-of-arms. A golden crown was set in place and a great sword belted about his waist.

Before Hodge's eyes, this old man was transformed into a striking figure—a king out of the stories of old, hale and hearty and ready to battle the evil of the world. In a rush of awe, Hodge bowed his head and knelt to the floor.

The king took a tottering step toward him. "My boy," he said, "I can barely breathe 'neath this mountain of iron."

CHAPTER TWENTY-NINE

*T*he transformation outside the tower walls rivaled that of King Alfred himself. When Hodge stepped out into the afternoon light, he could feel the difference.

Jayne jumped up from the stool on which she had been waiting. "Hodge!" she cried, but she stopped short upon seeing the king. "Y-Your M-Majesty." She dropped to a low curtsy, nearly falling over in her hurry.

With an easy gesture the king bade her rise, then turned to his High Chamberlain and Sir Champhries, who were waiting in the yard.

"Your Highness," Sir Champhries said, "all is ready. Our forces and those of Lord Roland will set out forthwith. The rest will follow within the week."

"Good. Bring about my horse. I will lead the advance."

"But Your Majesty—" began the Chamberlain.

The king cut him off. "Harry," he said, "my son will likely die tomorrow. I will not wait behind."

The Chamberlain bowed. "Yes, Your Majesty."

In a moment a silver-gray stallion was brought around, saddled and bridled and arrayed in the king's colors. The animal reminded Hodge of Bert, the warhorse. The two might have been foaled from the same mother.

Finally, and with a great deal of assistance from pages, the ostler, and several knights, the king was seated upon the stallion.

"Your Majesty," Hodge cried. "What about me?"

The Chamberlain put a hand on Hodge's shoulder. "Son, a battle is no place for an inexperienced youth."

"Nonsense," King Alfred said. "This youth has proven his mettle. Find him a mount."

Hodge's gratitude faltered before he had a chance to express it. "I . . . I don't know how to ride."

"I do," Jayne said. "We can ride together."

The king looked at her with an appraising eye. Then he winked. "Find *them* a mount," he said.

✦ ✦ ✦

By midafternoon the armies were well on the road to War-nick. Hodge and Jayne rode together on a skittish mare that jumped at every unexpected jangle and clatter. And in a large army on the move, there were many unexpected jangles and clatters.

"For all his size and strength," Jayne said, "Bert was much easier to manage."

"Aye, and thank heavens you'll not be going into battle with this one," said Sir Granby who rode along beside them. "You'll keep to the camp with us. We'll have the task of watching over the wagons and supplies and preparing for the wounded."

"Bah," said Sir William. "I'd rather be on the field. We owe Prince Leo a bit of something for what he did to us."

"He'll be handsomely paid," said Sir Granby. "We needn't fret over that."

"I'd just like to be one of them what's doin' the paying," said Brock, the youngest soldier of the group from Castle Marlby.

As the men spoke, Hodge found himself sympathizing with their words of revenge. Anger crept out from the hiding places in his mind to compete with his grief. He wished he were a soldier, too. He imagined himself standing at his full, unbound height, his leg healed, a sword in one hand, a shield in the other, towering above a fear-filled Prince Leo. "This is for deceiving me. This is for using me. This is for—"

But then he remembered the king's words: *My son will likely die tomorrow.* He shook his head.

"What's wrong?" Jayne asked.

"Nothing," Hodge answered. "Only . . . will there be anything after tomorrow?"

"I don't know. Nothing is as we hoped."

Perhaps there was one thing. "I'm still with you," Hodge said.

Together they rode along with the great army, on through the long afternoon and into evening. Just after nightfall, Hodge spied an owl passing overhead, off on its nighttime hunt. Curious about the noisy marchers below, it turned and glided over the column again.

The sight of the owl made the grief well up inside Hodge once more. And though this wasn't *his* owl, he whispered in a choking voice, "Good hunting."

✦ ✦ ✦

After a half-hour's rest at dawn, the armies took to the road again. Hodge's aching leg acted as a constant reminder of every mile that had passed, but as he told Jayne, he was becoming accustomed to the pain.

The morning's march led them into a dense forest, where the sound of their passage sent clouds of birds scolding through the branches. By noon, the woods thinned and finally gave way to the plains around Warnick. They had arrived, though perhaps too late. A haze of battle obscured the city and much of the surrounding field. For all Hodge could tell the city had already fallen.

But the royal armies did not falter. Quickly they spread out at the edge of the forest. The mounted knights divided and moved to either side of the ranks of foot soldiers, while rows of bowmen lined up behind. A trumpet signal echoed down the column, and the armies advanced.

"Now *we* set up shop," said Sir Granby. "Tents for the wounded. Beds for the battle-weary."

While the army had been organizing for the attack, the supply wagons were arranged on a rock-strewn hillside in good view of the field. Lackeys and workmen scurried about, setting up camp while Sir Granby's small band of soldiers barked orders. Hodge and Jayne sat atop one of the wagons and watched, glad to be free of their nettlesome mount.

Sir Granby reined in his horse beside the wagon. "King Alfred would not be prevented," he said. "See, he advances with his knights."

Hodge nodded, unable to take his eyes off the field.

"The city is burning," Jayne said. She pointed out flickers of red, just visible through the smoky haze.

"Hurry," Hodge silently urged. "Hurry."

Still the armies continued their slow advance.

"What are they waiting for?" he asked.

"Surprise," answered Sir Granby. "The enemy is not yet aware of them. They are too intent on the city."

Hodge squinted, trying to make out the enemy positions. "I can't see."

"There." Sir Granby pointed as a swirl of breeze exposed a siege tower poised before the city gates. "And there." He nodded toward a cadre of pikemen lined up for attack.

The armies of the king advanced. The afternoon breeze grew stronger. The obscuring haze lifted from the field, exposing the enemy positions. The city held out against the final attack, but it wouldn't last much longer. Trumpets blared across the field, and the king's mounted knights sprang forward. In an instant, the armies of Prince Leo were forced to face an unexpected onslaught.

The jarring sounds of the fight were audible to those watching from the hillside. The king's knights swept through the enemy foot soldiers, striking them down as they tried to reorganize for open battle.

"Where is the king?" Hodge asked. "Is he safe?"

"There," Jayne said, pointing to the left.

"See how his knights protect him," Sir Granby said.

Indeed, whenever the king broke through to face danger on the field, his men steered him away, keeping him on the outskirts of the fighting. But, as the battle intensified, he redoubled his efforts, charging here and there with a handful of knights following in his wake.

"He makes their duty difficult," Sir Granby added.

Hodge nodded. The king, in all his battle gear, formed

a majestic figure, even from a distance. "He's not like his son."

With the knights pressing in on either side, the enemy armies gathered toward the center of the field. It was then that the bowmen let fly their first barrage of arrows. The enemy fell in waves. Finally the king's foot soldiers attacked.

"We could be out there, too," Brock said as he approached the wagon. "By the time any of the injured are brought to us, there will be no one left to guard them from."

"Don't worry," said Sir Granby, "we'll have our chance."

✦ ✦ ✦

The battle raged on into the afternoon. Lord Pertwie's and Prince Leo's soldiers put up a desperate struggle. Though the king's army still had the advantage, it was no longer the simple rout Brock had bragged about.

"Lord Pertwie is a fool to keep fighting," Brock said.

"Wait," Jayne cried, standing up in the wagon. "Look at the city. What is happening there?"

A stream of people poured from the gates. "What are they doing?" Hodge asked.

"It's the city garrison," Sir William said, "joining in the fight."

"It's more than that," Sir Granby added. "Must be the whole city itself."

The people rushed from the gates, forming a wall that

pressed forward against the armies of Prince Leo and Lord Pertwie.

"They're done for now," Brock said.

It appeared his words were true. There was no longer a clear delineation between the attackers and the attacked. In the midst of the melee, a band of horsemen broke clear and raced across the plain. The king's knights were still engaged and unable to give pursuit.

"We should go after them," Brock said.

"No," said Sir Granby. "Our duty is here. Besides, it appears they are coming to us."

While Hodge watched, the fleeing group altered its course and now galloped toward the camp.

Sir Granby stood up in his stirrups and shielded his eyes with his hand. "I told you we'd have our chance. To your mounts, men. Hodge, you and Jayne get under the wagon. Keep hidden. You'll be safe there."

Hodge was slow in obeying. "Who are they?" he asked. But Sir Granby had already ridden off.

The lackeys and workmen scattered, fleeing into the woods.

"Hodge, come on." Jayne pulled him down from the wagon. "Under here."

He ducked behind the wheels and squirmed his way to the other side where he could get a view down the hill. He shuddered. Sir Granby's force was outnumbered by more than half.

CHAPTER THIRTY

*B*rock was the first to fall. A blow from a mace sent him crashing to the ground with his horse on top of him. Sir William avenged the young soldier with a thrust of his sword, but then two horsemen crowded him close and dragged him from his mount. Forced back to the wagons, The remaining soldiers made a brave stand. They wheeled their horses about and charged the enemy, unseating several, only to be driven back into the camp. One by one they were struck down. Sir Granby was the last to fall.

Hodge and Jayne huddled together beneath the wagon and watched in horror.

"Oh, Hodge . . ."

"Shhh. Maybe they won't see us."

But an enemy rider reined his horse to a stop and dismounted. He dragged the injured Sir Granby to his feet.

"Where is King Alfred?" the man roared. "His colors are here. *Where* is he?" It was Lord Pertwie.

"His Majesty is on the field," the old soldier said with a gasp. "He—he led the charge against you." Blood oozed from the corner of his mouth. His head lolled to the side.

"You lie. The king is no fool. He would not risk himself."

"*You* are the—"

Lord Pertwie shook him. "That's enough! I remember you from Castle Marlby. You were stubborn there as well." He pulled a dagger from his belt. "Now tell me, where is the king?"

Hodge could bear no more. Despite Jayne's attempts to hold him, he wriggled out from under the wagon. "The king is not here," he cried. "He's not a coward like you. He's on the field where he belongs, trying to repair what damage you have done."

Lord Pertwie let Sir Granby fall and turned his attention to Hodge. He pulled off his plumed helmet. "Look," he called over his shoulder. "It's your crippled tagalong."

Bareheaded and armorless, Prince Leo sat astride a jet-black warhorse within the remaining handful of enemy soldiers. Hodge felt a hot blaze inside him at the sight of the prince, enough to overpower any fear he might have had of Lord Pertwie.

"You are all cowards," Hodge cried, spitting the words at the prince. He ducked in time, and Lord Pertwie's blow glanced off his shoulder.

The man glared at him. "Now you will pay."

"Leave him be," Prince Leo said. "If he says the king is not here, he is not here. Hodge would not lie."

"This imp is responsible for our defeat this day! He must be punished."

Despite his injured leg, Prince Leo was off his horse in an instant. "You heard what I said."

"Yes, I heard." Lord Pertwie's voice dropped to a threatening whisper. "But I will do as I please."

Prince Leo limped toward him. "Not while I have breath."

Lord Pertwie laughed. "You have been bewitched by a common dog."

"That may be. Let him go."

Lord Pertwie lunged at the prince.

"Run," Prince Leo cried as he dodged the blade. "Get out of here."

But Hodge didn't stir. He knew he should obey, but like the soldiers around him he watched in amazement as the two men grappled for the knife.

The prince pulled Lord Pertwie to the ground. A memory stirred in Hodge's mind, a recollection of what Prince Leo had said long ago when teaching him chess—something about how a more powerful piece could protect a Pawn. Maybe the opposite was true, too. He broke free of his paralysis and picked up a rock.

A groan escaped the prince. Lord Pertwie staggered to his feet.

"Get away from him!" Hodge cried. He snatched up another rock.

Lord Pertwie raised his head. "Now for you." He shifted his grip on the knife.

Hodge cocked his arm back.

Lord Pertwie chuckled. "Ah, a mighty warrior." But he never said another word. He dropped to the earth, felled by Hodge's first stone.

Hodge turned to the remaining soldiers, ready to let fly the second stone, but the soldiers made no move. They glanced from Lord Pertwie to the prince, both lying motionless on the ground. They looked to the city where the battle continued. Then without speaking they turned their horses about and rode off toward the woods.

Jayne clambered out from beneath the wagon and hurried to Sir Granby. "Hodge, he's dead."

Hodge nodded. He dropped the rock. His hands felt thick and clumsy, and a dizziness swept through his head. His legs threatened to collapse beneath him. He closed his eyes so he wouldn't have to see the faces of those who had fallen because of him—Lord Selden, Tom Dalby, Sir Granby, Fleet. . . .

A voice cut through his anguish. "Hodge," it whispered. "Yet again, you've saved me."

He looked up. Prince Leo had struggled to a sitting position, his hand clutched to his stomach.

Jayne was already at his side.

"Shhhh," she said. "Rest easy."

✦ ✦ ✦

Evening had fallen by the time Hodge and Jayne had made Prince Leo more comfortable. They didn't dare move him, but they had been able to stanch his wound and stop the bleeding with bandages from the surgeon's pavilion. None of the workmen or lackeys had returned, so Hodge and Jayne had to make do themselves.

"Thank you, Lord Hodge," Prince Leo said, when Hodge offered him a cup of water.

"Don't call me that. You know I don't like to be teased."

"Please, let me have my little fantasy. If Pertwie may be called *Lord*, then certainly you can, too. Or better."

Prince Leo drank from the cup, though it appeared more water dribbled through his beard than was swallowed. "I thought you would like to know," he said, "Cull and Wat are safe. Lord Pertwie was not happy, for you took his horse. But I insisted."

"He was a fine horse," Jayne said.

The night air was turning chill. Hodge hesitated to

start a fire for fear the scattered enemy soldiers would be attracted by the light, so he wrapped blankets around the prince to try and stop his chattering teeth.

"Perhaps I'll never see those wondrous caves of yours," he said when Hodge settled down beside him and Jayne. "Tell me more about them."

"Why?"

"Because they sound spectacular."

"No. Why did you . . . ?" But now Hodge wasn't sure which question he really wanted to ask.

Prince Leo shivered and pulled his blankets closer. "Because I am a scoundrel."

Hodge shook his head. That wasn't the answer he was looking for. "A scoundrel wouldn't have risked his life to save me."

The prince shrugged, then winced at the pain it caused him. "You reminded me of someone."

He eased himself back to stare at the night sky. "This world is an ancient place," he said, "though I believe the stars are much older. It makes me tired just to think of it. I do believe I'm ready to let it go."

The prince's words left an unsettled feeling in Hodge's chest. "What do you mean?"

"Did you know I had a brother?" Prince Leo asked. Before Hodge could answer he continued. "Younger than me, he was. About your age, Hodge. But not as strong as you. I tried to teach him to be strong, but he preferred games of strategy. I insisted he learn the sword and the mace. He taught me chess." He paused to cough, a dry rattling cough that shook his shoulders and made him grimace with pain.

"Shhh," Jayne whispered. "That's enough."

Prince Leo pulled at his unkempt beard. "Did you know the king hates me?"

"No. He couldn't."

"Oh, but he does. 'Twas my sword that pricked my brother. Such a tiny wound, yet not even the king could save him. Not even my father. Such is the power of a king." He closed his eyes. "I think I'll rest now."

Soon his chest rose and fell with the steady rhythm of sleep, with neither a cough nor a rattle in his breath.

"Do you think he'll be all right?" Hodge asked.

"He will now," Jayne said.

CHAPTER THIRTY-ONE

*I*n the early morning Hodge awoke to the sound of horses. He and Jayne jumped to their feet and stood protectively over the prince, but their fear was unfounded. It was Lord Roland and his men.

"What has happened here?" Roland asked, dismounting with a rattle and clink of chain mail.

"Lord Pertwie tried to kill the prince," Hodge answered.

Lord Roland removed his helmet and knelt to pull back the blanket covering the prince's face. "It seems he has succeeded," Roland said. "King Alfred must be informed."

"Wh-what?" Hodge stammered.

Roland signaled to one of his men. "Find the king. Bring him here." The man rode off at a gallop.

"Now, tell me what happened."

It took Hodge a moment to realize Roland was speaking to him. With stumbling words he told what had taken place, with Jayne filling in when he faltered.

"You may go now," Roland said at last, dismissing them as if they were but servants reporting the inventory of the castle stores.

While the soldiers took care of the casualties with respectful efficiency, Hodge and Jayne moved out of the way. The blue light of morning spread across the plain. Autumn mists wisped up from the dew-laden grass to replace the smoke of burning from the day before. A lark sang from the forest behind them, its lilting song big enough to fill the whole world.

Hardly able to explain his feelings to himself, Hodge had a sudden urge to be as far away as possible when the king arrived.

"Come on," he said to Jayne. "I want to see the city up close."

Without a word she followed him down the hill. They took a wandering course toward Warnick, trying to avoid the worst of the battle remnants scattered across the field. As the morning warmed with the rising sun, movement increased upon the road that led to the city, until a crowd had assembled, milling about as if awaiting something. Hodge limped as he led Jayne across the battle-trampled grass.

"It appears the city has survived," Hodge said with relief when they were close enough to clearly make out the walls and towers.

"Though not without injury," Jayne said. "Look." She pointed at the blackened stone and smoldering rooftops.

"But we came in time," he said. "We came in time."

Jayne clasped his hand. "Yes, Hodge. We did."

He kept her hand in his, and together they moved to join the gathering crowd. "What's happening?" he asked.

A grizzled old man with a blood-encrusted ear turned to him. "The king is coming, with all his heroes," he said. "The battle is won!"

An expectant hush fell upon the field. A rustle of whispers swept over the crowd, and then that, too, was quieted. Despite his earlier feelings, Hodge couldn't keep down his own excitement. He squeezed Jayne's hand. The trumpet fanfare that rolled across the plain might have been sounding within Hodge's own heart.

Jayne stood on her toes and peered back along the road. "Look!"

The morning sun glinted off the plumed helmets of the mounted standard bearers as they approached on white stallions. Their polished armor shone like a new day dawning. Hodge wondered if these knights had even fought in the battle of the day before. It was as if they had been reserved for this moment.

A cheer went up from the crowd, as the people parted to make way for the royal passage.

Hodge strained to catch a glimpse of the king, but it wasn't until he was right upon them that Hodge saw his burden. King Alfred, still arrayed in his battle dress, rode slowly by, carrying the lifeless body of Prince Leo in his arms.

"I'm sorry, Your Majesty," Hodge cried, though he doubted the king could hear him through the cheering of the throng. But the royal head turned, and the royal eyes met Hodge's. The king's eyes were blue, the same striking blue as Prince Leo's. But instead of reminding Hodge of ice on the Eiderlee, they reminded him of the morning sky.

The king bowed his head to Hodge, as a man would bow to an equal.

✦ ✦ ✦

The royal procession passed, but much of the throng poured onto the road and followed.

"Prince Leo tried to save us," Hodge said, after the king and his son had disappeared from their view.

"Yes," Jayne said.

The last of the knights passed through the gates.

"I don't understand. Why would he do it for us?"

"He did it for you, Hodge. I believe he cared for you. Even Lord Pertwie could tell that."

246

As the crowd began to disperse, Hodge noticed many more who had been injured in the fighting.

"But why?"

"You reminded him of his brother."

A tall youth just across the way had to be supported by his companions. His head was bandaged with a blood-stained cloth. There was something familiar about him. Hodge stepped into the road.

"Where are you going?" Jayne called.

"Fleet?" Hodge cried.

The injured youth raised his head and focused on Hodge with difficulty.

"Fleet?"

The young man tried to pull away from those who held him.

Hodge caught his brother just as he was about to fall. "Oh, Fleet! I've been searching forever! I thought you were—"

"Hodge," Fleet gasped. "Is—is that you?"

"Yes, it's me." Hodge lowered his brother to the ground.

Bells began to peal within the city, joyously announcing the arrival of the king. Their bright sounds rang out into the sky, sending birds spiraling from the rooftops.

Fleet feebly clasped his brother's arm. "I didn't know where to find you. I didn't know where else to look. So I came here. But now I'm afraid I've been wounded sore.

My head and my insides. It hurts, Hodge. I fear I may be dying."

Hodge helped Fleet lie back. He cradled his brother's head in his arms and whispered, "Everything will be all right now. I'm here to take care of you."

The ringing bells continued, echoing up into the clouds that billowed over the plain. Hodge stroked his brother's brow. The dispersing crowd looked down at them with curiosity.

"Who *is* he?" the grizzled old man asked Jayne, pointing at Hodge.

"Just a commoner," she answered. "Like you and me."

The old man shook his head. "I thought he might be one of King Alfred's heroes," he said, "but for his crooked back."

Jayne laughed her bright, sparkling laugh—a sound Hodge thought was more beautiful than the bells.

"What crooked back?" she said.